Camille Juteau

# Moonlit Sins

By

Camille Juteau

**MOONLIT SINS**

Camille² Juteau

# Copyrights

# Credits

Story By: Camille Juteau

Proofreader: Logy Hebdon

Illustration By: TigerDrop


Title Logo Artist: IvanMichael12

# Chapter 1: The Night Hunt

*The Moonlit Sins have been unleashed on the world at the beginning of times. They are demons. They existed long before men and beasts. The sins infected generations after generations. Cursing men and women alike for the rest of all eternity and plaguing everyone with grave weaknesses...*

*However, these demons... These sins, unfortunately, cursed a small group of special people a bit more than the others. Choosing them. Today, only a handful of random people are cursed by these sins.*

*Oh, and want to know why these strange sins were called the Moonlit Sins?*

*It's because they were affected by the moon.*

*The moon shows these sins for what they truly are and turns their wearers into monsters. Beasts.*

Hunting in the dark gave her a feeling of power and a sense of skill.

However, little did she know that she wasn't the only one hunting tonight...

To be truthful, she wasn't even hunting so much because the reality of it was that she was the one being hunted...

This beautiful and strong young woman who went by the name of *Maleva* was, indeed, the one getting prowled on.

All of a sudden, something abruptly stopped on her trek in the middle of the woods as she was running through the thick bushes—she felt a presence. It was dark. There was something behind her.

"Who's following me?" The young woman declared with a proud and confident tone in her voice.

...

Nothing came out of it, at first.

"Show yourself!" She said, louder and more determined.

A couple of bushes were then shuffled... Something or someone soon came out of those bushes... A dark silhouette appeared and slowly came closer to her...

... It was revealed that a boy—a young man, had been following her all along. Not necessarily hunting, really, but following her, at least.

The young man coming out of hiding not only made it so she could see him but also, so *he* could see her better. Much better.

Finally able to see her well for the first time that night, he witnessed the true beauty of this eighteen-year-old woman with a heavily developed body. Incredibly voluptuous with generously soft, squishy, and huge breasts that were constantly jiggling whenever she moved. A large and perfectly rounded ass, which could partially be seen from the front as well. Thick, jumbo, and juicy thighs. She possessed the thickness of the body of a big and beautiful woman while still being fit and muscular. In shape. She had it all, and it was all-natural, too.

He came closer to her, so she could see her better.

The name of this young man was no other than *Michael*.

"Oh, *Michael?* It's you... What are you doing here, so far away from the village?" She asked him.

"I wanted to come hunt with you," he explained to her.

"Ah..." She squinted. "... But I already told you that it was too dangerous at night. I am the only one in the village who can hunt at night without any issue. You can't stay here. You have to go back."

"Don't talk down to me like I'm a kid because I'm not, okay?"

"That's not what I said, at all. You have no experience in hunting, and I do, so go back to the village right away."

"Then, how am I supposed to gain experience if I can't get some during real hunts, huh?" He asked her.

"Oh, you can obtain as much experience as you want, but not during dangerous hunts past midnight. That's for me to do."

"I don't care, I want to hunt with you tonight—"

—*Creak!*

They both heard a branch cracking behind them!

"Shut up! What is this?" She stopped everything and turned around as fast as she possibly could...

... Behind them!

They were a pair of wolves!

Real quadruped wolves with bright yellow eyes.

Foam at the mouth.

Fangs out.

It was true, tonight, she wasn't the one hunting... They were hunting her, instead...

"Maleva! Look out!"

The two common wolves went for her!

They wanted her throat! They attacked in order to kill her immediately, so they could eat it as fast as possible. That was what they thought was going to happen, but unfortunately for them, she wasn't a regular young woman. Maleva was by far the best huntress in their village, and she was able to respond to their attack before it was too late.

She smirked.

In a flash—she took out a sharp and huge dagger she was hiding this entire time underneath her ultra-mini skirt. This dagger was no ordinary blade, it was a knife, and it was a kunai. A sharp dagger with a rounded tip. She took it and immediately swung at the two wolves! Two slashes! Two cuts!

The pair of wolves couldn't complete their assault and instead came crashing down on the ground! They were already long dead once they landed on the ground. They soon stopped moving.

Maleva had already defeated the two wild wolves.

"You... Cut them down pretty easily..."

"Now, do you understand why these woods are such a dangerous place at night, huh?" Maleva asked him, as she quickly washed her blade from the blood of the wolves and placed her weapon away. Once again, hidden under her skimpy skirt.

"Not too bad. I reckon that you're pretty talented with a blade, but I still personally prefer rifles and pistols rather than simple daggers and swords."

"Look. I don't care. Blades work better in my own opinion. They get the job done," she shut him down right before...

*... Growl!*

"What?" Maleva barely had enough time to turn around to realize that one of the two wolves she just killed had somehow survived her deadly slashes. One of the wolves seized this opportunistic distraction to leap at her and attempt to bite her fragile neck one more time!

Maleva tried pulling her dagger back out, but it was too time... She wouldn't make it. She, unfortunately, couldn't defend herself.

She was going to perish right here... Right now...

*Bang!*

Unless?

One bullet between the two eyes and the wolf went down again! This time, dead for good. The wolf stopped moving again.

Maleva turned back around in sheer confusion. She saw hot smoke coming out of the tip of the cannon of a pistol. A pistol the young man was holding in his right hand. He, then, blew the smoke away.

"You were saying?"

She sighed.

"Lucky shot..."

"Lucky shot? Are you serious? Could you at least thank me for saving your life?"

"Saving my life? Are you kidding? I was fine. I am always fine on my own. You should know that."

"Always a lone wolf as I can see?" he pointed out to her.

"I slay wolves. I'll never be one," she corrected him as she folded her arms together, right underneath her huge tits.

"Sure. Whatever. Do you still want me to go back to town?"

"Well... You just proved your worth, so I guess you can stay during the hunt to assist me if you insist... But only to assist me! Understood?"

"Understood," he nodded.

"Now that we cleared this area of those wolves, we should be able to hunt in peace for a little while, now... We'll be able to hunt a few boars and perhaps a deer, even if we're fortunate enough. This way..." She led the path.

"Following you."

*Her name is Maleva, and I've had a serious crush on her for the longest time... Ever since I was a kid, in fact. Going on a hunt like this with her was something that I had been hoping for a while. I finally had a shot at working side-by-side with her. Proving my worth. I am not going to screw this up!*

"What are you doing? Come on..."

Maleva called for him. Quickly snapping him out of this dreamy trance he was in.

"Right..."

He followed her. For good, this time.

As the two trekked deeper into this darker and vastly more dangerous area of the woods surrounding the small town where they both lived, they soon began to feel observed...

It wasn't just a feeling. They were truly being watched by some obscure forces.

It was time for the two of them to prepare for the worst.

Maleva pulled a few more kunai from underneath her skirt. She had more.

One alarming wolf howled in the far distance later, and Maleva suddenly felt enthralled by the alluring phantoms of the deep forest. As the howl reached her ears and settled into her mind, she was soon overtaken by an abrupt sense of arousal. The deeper she had gotten into the woods, the more aroused she was getting... She attempted to conceal it, but it was overwhelming. Even for someone as strong as her.

*I'm convinced I can make it! I can become the greatest hunter of our region and keep our town safe! Then, when I gain enough experience, I'll seduce and marry Maleva! I'm destined to marry her! I know it!*

# Chapter 2: Two Hunters

In the heart of the woods, the hunt truly began!

More howling could be heard in the far distance.

The deeper they ventured into the dark woods, the more howling they could hear, and the louder and more menacing it was also becoming.

"You sure you're cut out for this, Michael?"

"This again? I am a much better hunter than you believe me to be. Trust me. I'll definitely show you," the young man confronted Maleva once more.

"Sure..."

*I don't really know what it is... Huh... I feel so strange. The more time I spend in the woods tonight the warmer it gets. It typically isn't like this. It doesn't make any sense. It's typically much colder at this hour and at this time of the year. And for some reason, I feel drawn to him... I don't know why, but I want to be standing a bit closer to him. It started earlier when he first came out of the bushes. He's just as warm as I am. If not hotter. He smells great, as well. I never thought I'd feel that way. I also feel like I am blushing. It's crazy. Is that... My nipples hardening for some reason? What's going on with me all of a sudden?* Maleva asked herself as she was still at the head of this duo of hunters. Still leading the hunt.

"Maleva, are you alright?" Michael finally asked her, as he had been observing her walking a bit odd for the past few minutes. Walking a bit more sloppily than usual. Not like a huntress.

"What? Yeah. Why?" She kept walking forward, but did turn to him. Turned out that she was blushing even more now.

"Don't know. You were walking a bit weirdly. Wait. Hold on. Why are you blushing all of a sudden?" He questioned her.

"I... Don't... Know..."

"Are you sick or something?" Michael asked her.

"Would you like to take a short rest or something...? We have been scouting these parts of the woods for the last, few hours now... We should take a break..." She suggested.

"Sure. Why not?"

***

"Too bad we can't have a bonfire during such a dangerous hunt..." Michael remembered.

"We don't need a bonfire to warm ourselves up since you're already around..." She mentioned to him, as she blushed, accidentally letting something slip out.

"What?" A huge amount of confusion overwhelmed him.

"N—Nothing..." She quickly looked the other way.

"Is there something you want to tell me?" He asked her.

"It's just that... I don't know what's going on with me... I've been feeling strange since earlier... My body feels so hot all the time... And... And... I feel like I want to give you a hug..." She admitted.

"A hug? You don't seem like the type of person who enjoys giving and receiving hugs, but sure... Why not?" The young man accepted her request and gave her one big hug. Maleva enjoyed it so much that she blushed even more during that physical contact. Meanwhile, Michael enjoyed it just as much as her, if not more. He felt her huge and ultra-soft pillows. Which served as breasts, rubbing against his chest.

The gorgeous, young woman with emerald green eyes couldn't stop staring at him during and following the big hug.

Her long hair was mostly red with a couple of green streaks, resulting in the two colors fusing a lot and making it look brown in a couple of different spots. Her pale, white skin was beautifully glowing due to the influence of the moon in the dark sky.

Her huge *34M Cups* boobs remained squished against his chest for the longest time... Maleva had quite a completely voluptuous body. The big tits—as previously mentioned. The wide and seductive hips. The large ass, as well as the long and thick thighs.

Quite frankly, Maleva wasn't wearing enough clothes or something exactly her size for the torrid and thick body she had. However, what she wore clearly showcased what the young and virgin woman had to offer.

Her outfit mainly consisted of a fishnet top, as well as a pair of fishnet stockings. The three pieces were red and green. The same colors as the revealing and sleeveless top she wore over her chest. A top, which ended in an ultra-mini skirt. A skirt that did not even cover her crotch and her orange thong. She also had red and green nipple covers under the fishnet top, made in the shape of dog or wolf paws. Black high-heeled shoes on her feet.

Finally, she also had thin glasses over her eyes, so she could see and hunt as well as she always did.

Meanwhile, there also was the young man...

Michael was a young man eighteen years old with unusually pale, white eyes and medium-length dark brown hair.

He wore a gray outfit fabricated of various animal furs that he pieced together.

"May I kiss you, now?"

Then, before even waiting for his opinion on the matter, she leaned forward and went ahead and kissed him. Right on the lips.

A seductive kiss, left Michael wanting a lot more.

He received a lot more as she soon inserted her long tongue inside his mouth, making this a much sexier kiss than he anticipated.

"What's going on?" The young boy was finally able to ask her once their erotic kiss ended.

"What? You don't like it?" All of a sudden, Maleva blushed more than ever... Deeply beginning to feel like he wasn't interested in doing things of that nature with someone such as her.

"No! It's not it! I love it! I swear! It's just that it happened so fast and I had no idea that you were interested in me in the first place..."

"I didn't even know myself to be honest... I don't know how this came to be, but I want to do more with you, Michael. Do you mind if I get naked for you, now?" She offered to him with a light tone in her voice.

"I mean..."

... The young man was just about to tell her that she could totally do this for him when a strange stomping noise was suddenly heard behind them...

Everything stopped.

Michael was the first one to pause everything and turn his head around. Then, when she noticed that something was off, Maleva did as well.

Before they knew it, another wolf stalked them and jumped at them! Judging from the look of it, this beast, which was much bigger than the two other ones from earlier, meant to attack Maleva and her alone. Leaping at her! Attempting to maul her throat.

"No!"

However, at the last second, Michael swiftly jumped and placed himself between her and the animal!

He stopped it!

But, this also meant that instead of biting Maleva, the fierce wolf bit him! It mauled his right arm!

Taking a serious chunk out of it!

"Ahn!" Michael screamed in pain.

"Michael!"

It was too late. He had already been bitten.

Blood was drawn.

The wolf eventually let go of his arm and then escaped into the forest.

Michael collapsed on the ground and fainted not too long after saving Maleva's life.

"Michael?"

He was done for.

They were now so deep in the woods that they were too far away to come back to their village, now... It was going to take too long to bring him back by carrying him. She had to think of something else. She had to find something else.

# Chapter 3: The Awakening

Perhaps Michael would continue breathing for the next couple of hours.

Or perhaps he still had a few days left.

Who knew?

It was the next morning and thankfully, Maleva had somehow managed to find a random wooded cabin somewhere in the middle of the forest, which was perfect since they were too far to come back to the village like this.

It was unlocked, so she was able to bring him inside. There was even a comfortable bed in there that was simply perfect for him to rest on. However, Michael was still unconscious.

Maleva managed to stop the bleeding on his arm and applied a bandage to it, but that was about it. She wasn't a doctor. She wasn't a healer. She was a hunter.

*There's nothing more I can do for him. We need food, so I better leave him to rest here while I go hunting... He'll need something to eat when he wakes up... If he does...* Maleva thought to herself as she observed the young man breathing hard on the bed.

"Might as well go do what I do best..." Maleva mentioned out loud before turning her heels and heading out the door.

***

*Thump! Thump!*

Maleva shot two kunai and two deer came down.

Hunting was good that morning.

Well, that part of the hunt went well at least, because something else came up... On her way back, as she pulled the pair of deer by their legs because she was that strong of a woman. She felt a presence... Almost as if someone or something was watching her in the woods. She felt the exact same thing last night when the last wolf suddenly attacked them and bit Michael's arm. Just the same as last night, it didn't feel like the presence of a regular wolf, but rather something bigger, darker, and a lot more menacing...

Something was definitely here with her.

This uneasy and nervous feeling of being watched by this presence thankfully became lesser and lesser as she made it back to the wooden cabin, where she left the injured Michael.

***

Maleva left the two deer in the shed right beside the cabin for now while she hurried to go check on Michael and his current situation.

The young woman opened the door of the cabin and stepped inside to discover that Michael was no longer in bed. She looked around... Michael was nowhere to be seen.

"Michael?"

Maleva stepped forward and moved deeper into the cabin, exploring it a bit more. Where was he? Michael had vanished. She couldn't find him anywhere.

"Michael, where are you?"

Then, all of a sudden, hidden behind the front door and the shadows of the cabin, appeared Michael. He was right behind her, sneaking up on her. She didn't know anything. Michael was preying on her, just like a wolf would do with their meal.

"Maleva..." He whispered her name right before making his move on her and seizing her from behind. She never suspected anything. He swallowed her whole with his arms and immediately went for the throat. Rushed for it. He began by licking her neck.

"Huh? Michael! Is that you?" She asked him.

*It's him! He snuck up on me! I can't believe it! No one has ever gotten the best of me like this! I never get surprised like this! What's going on?* Maleva thought to herself right before the young man rushed to kiss her on the lips. She wasn't expecting that, as well.

"What are you doing?" She asked him after the sudden kiss concluded.

Still behind her, Michael pushed Maleva against one of the walls of the cabin and proceeded to push her orange underwear down. Slightly undressing her. Not too much, just enough so he could push his huge and hard cock against her pussy lips.

"What's taking over you?" She continued asking time and time again what was going on.

His erect cock soon entered her vagina, and he began fucking her! It was pure, raw, and incredibly sloppy.

"Michael! Michael! Michael! Michael! This feels so good! This feels so good, Michael!" Maleva was already moaning, and her pussy lips were already lustfully wet. She was dripping wet, in fact, she was enjoying herself so much.

Her tongue was sticking out of her mouth and she was showing this ridiculously over-excited and over-aroused expression on her face while she was being fucked from behind by Michael.

The only piece of clothing that had sort of come off of her was her underwear. All the rest of her clothes were still on her. However, her soft and huge tits were aggressively bouncing so much in the air that they were threatening to fly out of her top.

Maleva was so much larger than him that it almost felt like Michael was attempting to mount something. She was taller and larger than him. Yet, he was more than capable of getting the job because the young woman's moaning soon intensified into a beautiful erotic crescendo.

"Ahn! This is my first time, Michael! My first time! I never had sex before! I'm coming! I'm coming, Michael!" It was true, her pussy couldn't handle this any longer, and she came without foreseeing it herself at all.

"Grrr..." Meanwhile, Michael growled and grunted as he suddenly pulled out of her tight and wet pussy and ejaculated all over the exterior of her pussy. Almost as if this wasn't the right moment for him to cum inside of her. In the end, her entire backside was covered in thick ropes of pure, white semen.

During sex, something changed with Michael. Something else. Something about him physically. During his ejaculation, his nails began growing. They became longer and much sharper. His nails turned into claws, and he accidentally slashed Maleva's large and exposed ass with both of his hands, creating deep claw marks on both sides of her ass.

This never seemed to hurt her.

If anything, it made her moan a bit more even.

As the young man finished ejaculating, he howled like a wolf.

It was not too long after that, they both heard another howl, responding to him. This second wolf howl came from outside. This was a beast, who was tracking them in the woods. It was the same one that attacked them and bit Michael's arm last night for sure. It was the same type of howl.

"Michael... What's going on? Why are you howling all of a sudden? Wait a minute... Did you just scratch me or something?"

# Chapter 4: Desired Warmth

It had become dusk.

It was Maleva's turn to be sick now.

They were both sick, but somehow, Michael's sickness appeared to have lessened a bit and was replaced by rage and sheer aggressiveness instead. With the way he treated Maleva earlier, he had mysteriously turned a lot rougher.

Maleva did try to take care of him when he was on the brink of dying, but was he going to do the same for her? Was he going to take care of her, as well?

First, Michael was bitten by this giant wolf as he was attempting to protect her. Then, he became sick. Michael clawed Maleva's backside earlier, and, now, she was the one who was dying.

Without Michael's help, Maleva still managed to make it back to the only bed in the cabin. She had to crawl her way up to the bed because of how tired she felt after what he had done to her... Including the surprise sexual intercourse (which she didn't mind, at all), and his clawing her, but she still made it work...

Barely breathing, she tried resting.

Meanwhile, Michael, or rather what was left of him, curled up in one of the corners of the cabin and couldn't stop himself from shaking.

His body was overheating.

He didn't know why.

"What's happening to me?"

It wasn't just a bad feeling... Something quite awful was happening to him, and it wasn't only his nails becoming sharper and shifting into claws.

It wasn't only his body that was changing.

It was also his mind.

Michael was progressively turning into a more aggressive and dominant young man. His body was only following suits. His claws became worse than before. They became longer. Sharper. Deadlier.

Then, it was his teeth. They turned shaper, as well. Almost as if all of his teeth were fangs now.

But there was more... As Michael's body was changing and getting twisted, he soon became hairier, as well. Before, Michael's face wasn't hairy, at all... Now he was growing a beard, and he was getting sideburns.

"I feel like my insides are burning up!" He shouted in that one corner of the cabin.

*Panting... Panting... Panting...*

He panted so much...

It wouldn't stop...

"Michael...? Michael...? Michael, where are you...? I need you, Michael..."

He heard her voice.

Her soft voice brought him back to reason, and finally, he could think of something other than his dire situation.

"Mal?" He called her by that shortened name. Too tired and sick to say her full name.

"Michael... Come to me... I need you, please... Come to me..." Feeling guided by her, he was drawn to her. This animalistic alteration of Michael ended up crawling from his corner of the cabin to her. He joined her in bed.

"How are you feeling?" He wished to know.

"Cold... So cold... Please, help me... Please, warm me up..."

"I can deal with that..." He confessed to her as he surrounded her thick body with his strong arms and brought her closer to his chest. He smoothly enveloped her.

He ended up warming her up in no time.

Michael's body was so warm, now that he was like a walking and talking bonfire at this point. Feeling her wondrous body against his was also more than enough to get him going. Michael was turned on in no time. His big cock ended up throbbing and hardening in less than a minute after joining Maleva in bed. Pretty quickly, his boner rubbed against her lower back. She felt it. She felt all of it.

"Is that you, Michael?"

"It's me..." He communicated with her with a deep and inhuman voice.

"Thanks for staying with me..."

"Do you want me?" This was the final frontier before he pushed the head of his cock inside of her pussy.

"I do..."

This was the last thing he needed.

*Clop!*

One microsecond later, the young man aggressively pushed his big cock inside of her vagina!

Her pussy lips were so wet that it was impossible for him to resist her. She was too succulent to turn down. Everything still felt so new. To the both of them, it didn't even feel like they just had sex earlier today. Both Michael and Maleva were left wanting more, even though they had already been satisfied earlier.

It was too bad that Michael didn't shoot his load inside of her pussy earlier. She would have been pregnant and this would have cemented his total dominance over her by him. But they weren't there just yet.

"Aw... Michael... Your cock..." She panted as he penetrated her.

"Maleva..."

"I want you to cum inside of my pussy this time..."

"That's what you really want?" Michael turned even harder once he heard this important piece of information.

"We've known each other since we were kids... Yet, this feels right to me... I want this... Who knows? Perhaps this is going to help me with this fever..."

"Mal. I don't think what you have is a fever."

"What do you mean?"

"I think it's something worse... Whatever it is..."

"Ahn! Oh, yes! Michael! This feels so good! Harder! Can you do me harder, please?" She begged him to go at it even stronger as he continued fucking her sideways in bed.

"I don't have a problem with that!"

"Aw! Yes! Yes! I'm coming! I'm coming! Please fill me up!"

"I will!" All of a sudden, Michael's voice turned deeper and more bestial. It was almost as if he growled at the same time as he attempted to speak.

"Aw! Ahn! I'm coming! I'm coming! You're making me come!"

"I'm filling you up!" He growled at her again.

Barely a couple of minutes after they finished, Michael pulled out of her, and Maleva drifted to sleep.

She was still sick.

Her life was still on the line.

The sickness didn't seem to go away, and this was not a fever, as Michael mentioned a bit earlier.

Yet, something that did go away after they finished fucking and that all semen was dumped into her, was Michael's current condition. Following his ejaculation, the claws became normal nails again... His wolf-like fangs decreased in size... He became less hairy... He was reverting to his normal self.

He looked like he was human again, somehow.

# Chapter 5: Howling At Midnight

A bit of time had passed, and it was now already nighttime.

It was midnight.

The wolves were howling again outside.

It felt like Michael and Maleva were taken as hostages inside the cabin by the legion of wolves outside, which were mostly never seen. Always hidden in dark shadows. Which made it a lot worse.

With Maleva still unconscious and sick, Michael ultimately decided to end this hostage situation and stand his ground.

"Screw this! I'm tired of these damned wolves!" He shouted as she stood up in the cabin. No longer afraid, Michael, who was back to his regular human form, decided to go outside! He slammed the door open and went outside to face the horde of beasts.

"Come face me! I'll beat your asses!"

Before he knew it, Michael was surrounded by the pack of wolves in the dark. They were waiting for him. They were expecting him to do something like this. Big mistake. It was one of the worst things he could have done. They circled around him. They were testing him before making their final and deadly move on him.

"I'm not scared! Come at me..."

However, the truth was that he was scared.

Slowly, but surely, they were about to attack him when—

—A certain someone suddenly showed up behind him.

He heard footsteps...

He turned around, and it was at that moment that he saw her... He saw Maleva standing there. Out of the cabin. Changed.

The wolves stepped back. They weren't expecting Michael to be ready to do battle with a partner. The wolves reevaluated everything and soon decided that it was better to leave for now, once they saw Maleva in her wolf form.

Michael saw it, too.

Maleva had awoken her wolf for the first time. She now had sharp claws, deadly-looking fangs, as well as red wolf ears coming out of her hair. She also had a red and green wolf tail on her back. Finally, the last physical change Michael observed was her eyes. Her irises were thin and sharp. Looking more animalistic and bestial than ever. Her emerald green eyes were a lot brighter than before, as well.

"Maleva...?"

The pack of wolves was now long gone...

She scared them away.

"What happened to you, Mal? How are you feeling?"

She slowly stepped closer toward him in the dark.

"I want you, Michael." She announced to him.

The young man looked behind him one more time and saw that there were no wolves around. All of them were gone. He then understood that Maleva did this.

"Mal... You're a wolf, now..." He pointed out to her.

"I... Feel... In... Heat..." It took her a long time to say this, but it had to come out. She had to tell him.

Too horny to contain herself, wolf Maleva jumped in the air and landed right on top of Michael, who had been lying down on his back for the past couple of seconds. The young man quickly ended up with her huge tits right in his face. Big and perfectly soft pillows just for him!

"Mal?"

Still too aroused to contain herself, she leaned forward to kiss him. She kissed him right on the lips before inserting her long and sensual tongue inside his mouth. Filling it up with her tongue. The young man accepted all of it without any issue. He was simply pretty surprised that he was getting to have that much sex with his crush in such a short period of time.

Not too long after they kissed with their tongues, Maleva lowered her top and pulled her big tits out for him. Now, her breasts were still inside her fishnet suit, but she had now completely removed the rest that was previously covering them. Wide and large areolas! Huge and thick nipples! All of it was right there in the young man's face!

"My breasts want you! Please suck on them!"

"If they want me so bad..."

Michael agreed to suck on her big tits right away. Her breasts couldn't wait to be sucked on, and it showed by the way her nipples were so erect.

The young man didn't even have to lean forward to suck on them. They were already right there in his face. So easy to access.

Michael sucked on the tit  on his right first. He sucked as hard as he possibly could before switching to the one on his left. Attempting to give equal attention and love to both of her nipples.

"Oh, yes... This feels so good... Finally, some relief..."

After he was done sucking on her tits, he had managed to make her so aroused and horny, that he knew exactly what was going to come next...

"I want to be bred by you again, Michael!"

"Bred by me?"

"Yes! I want your little puppies!" As she called them.

"Well, come over here, then..."

"But, I'm already on top of you!" That was the truth. She was already on top of him, so this was a lot easier that way. She only had to pull his big dick out of his pants and sit on it.

*Thump! Thump! Thump!*

She sat right on top of him and rode him!

Took control of him and they fucked once more!

"Yes! Yes! That's exactly what I wanted! I wanted your big cock in my wolf pussy again! Oh! I'm already about to come! I'm already coming!" She shouted at the top of her lungs, unable to be discreet. Now, everyone in these woods could hear them having sex.

*How did I manage to make her come this fast?* Michael wondered.

"I'm coming! I'm coming! Ahn! Yes! That's what I needed!" She continued moaning.

"I'm cumming, as well!"

"Good... Ahn! Ahn!"

"Do you still want me to empty my balls inside of you?"

"Yes! I wouldn't want it any other way!"

*She's even hornier as a wolf!*

"There it goes! I'm cumming inside of you!"

"I cannot wait to have your puppies!"

"Right..."

This still came across as pretty weird. Michael still couldn't believe that the both of them were turning into wolves.

The young man soon finished cumming inside of her, and she was still sitting on top of him. Still riding him.

Yet...

Something happened...

When Michael looked up, he realized that Maleva was turning back into a human.

# Chapter 6: Surviving The Hunting Ground

When the morning came and the dust settled a bit, the gravity of the situation they were in, was a lot clearer now

They had been attacked and both of them were turning into wolves.

Thankfully, both of them were in human form at the moment. It was almost as if the sickness that had been making them turn into wolves was gone for the time being.

"You know? This might have been the most terrible decision of your entire life... Do you know that?"

"What do you mean?"

"I went out for a midnight hunt. I always do that. It's the first time someone ever came with me and this happened... I told you not to come with me and to go back to the village, but no, you wouldn't listen, and now, we are both sick..."

"It's going to be okay. Don't worry about it."

"How can you be so calm?" Maleva asked him as the two of them trekked together through the woods. They voyaged as far as possible from that one cabin, since all of these dangerous wolves surrounded them and that this was no longer a safe place to be.

"Because I am not alone. I know we can survive and make it back to safety because we're together."

"Michael..."

"This way... I see something... There's something over there..."

"Perhaps it would be a great time for me to tell you what's truly going on around here..."

"What do you mean?"

"The real reason as to why I didn't want you to come with me at night for a hunt is the fact that I wished to protect you."

"Protect me?" Michael abruptly came to a full stop.

"It's something  I wasn't originally supposed to tell you about..."

"What is it?"

"You are the one most important person in our village. You always were." Maleva revealed to him.

"What's that supposed to mean? You're not making any sense, Mal?"

"You never realized it?"

"Realized what?"

"You are the only male in our village. And there's also something more to you that I can't reveal to you just yet... However, what I must tell you that is the most important thing right now is the fact that the wolves in this region are not normal wolves. You are not supposed to know about this, but the wolves in these woods are no animals—they are monsters. That's why I've been hunting them for so long. It's up to me to stop them before they destroy everyone..."

"Mal! Look out!"

However, it was already too late.

Maleva was sneakily and violently attacked by a shadowy force!

"Ugh!"

One blow in her back and she was sent flying in the air to the other side of the woods!

"Mal!"

She was down on the ground. Not moving.

Michael immediately meant to go up to her in the hope of helping her, but he was stopped by the same pack of wolves that surrounded them last night at the cabin. Turned out that's what just attacked Maleva in her back was them... The pack of wolves.

Michael was now completely surrounded by them.

"Uh! What do you want from us?" He asked them.

The pack of wolves then closed in on him.

He couldn't go anywhere. He couldn't escape.

Then, instead of synchronizing an assault on him, something pretty strange happened...

... All the wolves mysteriously combined with one another and formed some kind of monstrosity. A strange hybrid shape of all these wolves melted with one another.

This united transformation was required in order to reveal the true beast that was hiding underneath all this time.

The pack of wolves that had been after Michael and Maleva for the past couple of days was one big, bad wolf all along.

"What the hell is this?" Michael asked out loud, terrified of what he was seeing before his eyes. Quite frankly, he didn't really know what he was seeing. Ever since the pack of wolves showed up, it had been getting darker and darker here in the woods to the point of making it extremely difficult to see.

The only thing Michael was able to make out in the dark following the strange transformation, was the tall and large shape of one dangerous wolf standing on two feet. Staring straight at him.

"Mike... Run..." Maleva succeeded in whispering to him.

"No way. I can't leave you like this."

The werewolf howled one time as it turned completely dark outside and a full moon suddenly appeared in the sky.

The werewolf rushed toward Michael! Threatening to kill him!

"Run!" Maleva warned him one more time.

"I can't..."

*Slash!*

The bloodthirsty werewolf quickly reached Michael's position and suddenly attacked him! Slashing his chest with its claws!

"Michael!" Maleva grew incredibly worried about him.

The claws of the werewolf were now digging deep into his chest. Hurting him.

Everything became silent and no one moved for a certain period of time...

"Ugh..." The young man was in deep pain. He grunted a lot, but he was still standing.

"How are you not dead? It's okay. I'll make sure to destroy you before doing the same to your girlfriend over there." The werewolf finally spoke for the first time. Its voice was mysterious, to say the least. It was deep and dark, but it was entirely impossible to tell if its voice was male or female. The voice was monstrous and bestial.

"What did you just say...?" Michael murmured as he looked at his wound. He could see the claws digging into his chest, but for some reason, there wasn't much of an injury there.

Then...

... It was when it finally happened.

Michael began changing again.

Just like he did before and just like Maleva also recently did.

However, there was something different this time... This time, Michael would change completely into a werewolf.

The transformation was swift, and before they knew it, the young human had successfully turned into a tall and muscular werewolf, standing on two feet with a thick mocha brown fur all over his body.

His eyes were still white, but much brighter than ever before.

"Michael... No..." Maleva whispered.

"Another... Friend...?" The mysterious and savage werewolf asked.

"Grrrooooowlll!" Werewolf Michael lunged at his enemy before pulling his claws out of his chest and ultimately delivering a powerful blow with the claws of his right hand right at their face!

The attack was so strong that it defeated the enemy right away and also had the effect of ripping them to pieces by dividing the various wolves of the pack!

The wolves turned into dark shadows after getting separated!

Soon, they all vanished in the woods and this was the end of combat.

Werewolf Michael then soon turned to Maleva, who was still lying on the ground.

# Chapter 7: Dominating The Female

Michael didn't turn into a partial wolf, as he did before. This time, he was a complete werewolf.

When Michael finally turned to Maleva, who was still lying on the ground after getting attacked earlier, she was able to look up and observe something getting pushed out of the crotch of the beast.

She witnessed his werewolf's cock coming out of the interior of his body. The young huntress was shocked to see this at first, but ultimately made a lot of sense considering the fact that he had just evolved and transformed into this monstrous animal.

Throbbing right above her head, she saw Michael's werewolf dick, which was of a beautiful pink-red color.

He possessed a set of testicles that were the same pink-red color as his cock. This pair of balls were directly attached to his member, which was not so surprising. However, there was indeed something that was... In this bestial werewolf form, Michael was equipped with a second of the set of testicles. This second pair of balls was a bit more subtle and harder to see (especially at night or in the dark), but it was right there, hanging underneath his cock and his red balls.

This second set of testicles was covered in fur, while the others weren't. His dick had no foreskin. It was similar to a dog's dick but much bigger. Hence, he was a wolf and not a dog. His member was like a long tube with a couple of ridges on it, generously veiny as well, and a large and mushroom-like head. His glans was absolutely beautiful and looked both human-like and dog-like.

"Michael. What have you become?" Maleva was equally terrified and aroused by what she was witnessing.

"Grrrrhhh..." The werewolf growled at her right before pushing her onto the ground and forcing her to lie down on her back in the grass.

The young woman was then able to smell a strong dog smell in the air as she made physical contact with the animal, who used to be her childhood friend at one point in time.

Before she knew it, Maleva was on her back with her thick thighs spread apart.

The beast penetrated between her long and seemingly never-ending legs.

The tip of his reddish cock rubbed all over the exterior of her dripping wet pussy. Her clitoris was so sensitive that this erotic contact with this bestial member was more than enough to send electric shivers down her spine.

She purred as she soon realized what was going on and where this was heading...

The wolf was hunting tonight.

Missionary-style, he blasted his huge animal cock right inside of her human pussy. Maleva was still in her human form and this was exactly like this that she was the most vulnerable. She couldn't fight him off like this. Not while she was a human and that he was in this complete werewolf form. Not that she wanted to fight him off, to begin with.

No.

She welcomed this with open arms.

The werewolf pushed his big, bad cock as hard as possible against her wet and juicy vaginal lips until he was fully inside of her. His balls rubbed against the exterior of her butt-hole

"Michael... Yes... Do me..."

Maleva grew to moan so much that she was slurring her words every time she spoke.

Next up: The werewolf was so horny, that he suddenly ripped her fishnet top off of her body. Destroying it and pulling her big tits out in the open! Her nipples were still covered by nipple pasties in the shape of red and green wolf paws.

"Aw! Yes! Take them out! Use me and my boobs, you dominant animal!"

One second later, the werewolf had her left tit inside of his mouth and he was sucking it. Her thick and erect nipple was pretty deep into his mouth.

His long wolf tongue spun around her nipple. Stroking it.

"You're sucking so hard on it! This is making me so hot and wet!"

"Ooooowhoo!" The werewolf howled! Even with her nipple deep in his mouth as he savagely and passionately sucked on it.

All of this was happening at the exact same time he pushed his werewolf cock in and out of her erotically tight pussy.

Maleva was still a virgin not too long before this hunting trip they went on together.

Michael was the one who deflowered her.

Maleva never had sex before.

Michael was her only one.

This werewolf had such a big appetite and he soon switched breasts and sucked on her other nipple while continuing to blast her pussy.

Nothing could stop him.

She couldn't.

"Yes! Aw! Yes! I'm about to come! I'm about to come!"

"Growlll!" The creature growled at her again as he heard this.

"Oh! Um... Yeah... Aw! It's real! I'm really coming! I'm coming even harder than I have in the past couple of days during this hunting trip! I can't help it! Owwhhn! Aw! I'm coming!"

"Ouwlwnn!" The werewolf howled once more as he caused her to come.

This orgasm was the absolute pinnacle of everything that they were building toward. The best orgasm she had felt ever since she lost her virginity to her childhood friend, Michael.

Then, she felt it...

"Awn... Ufu... You're cumming too?"

He continued thrusting into her and demolishing her tight, little pussy. Exactly as she desired it to be the case.

"Yes, you are! You're cumming inside of me, you animal!"

He was.

The werewolf ejaculated deep into her pussy.

Filling her up without ever pulling out of her.

Maleva felt one thick rope of semen filling her up.

Two ropes of cum!

Three ropes!

And then a fourth!

The werewolf never pulled out of her, even long after he was done shooting his load in her, following the fourth rope of thick sperm.

Michael as the wolf was shaking...

He wouldn't pull out.

Almost as if he was stuck in her pussy.

"Michael? Are you stuck or something?" She asked him.

Then, it donned on her...

*Wait for a second! He's a wolf now! And just like a dog, does that mean that he knots a female's vagina in order to secure an impregnation with her?* Maleva thought to herself. Still aroused and overwhelmed by this sublime and imposing lust, she began panicking a bit.

# Chapter 8: So Far Away

"I want to know what the hell is going on here..." Michael announced to Maleva not too long after he finally transformed into a human.

As painful as it was.

Michael had never felt pain on this level before. This was entirely unlike anything else.

"Are you going to be alright?" Maleva asked him as she helped him move forward in the woods, desperately attempting to find home again. It felt so long since the last time they saw the village where they both lived.

Maleva knew these parts of the woods like the back of her hand, yet the forest no longer looked, nor felt like the same place anymore. It could have been because she was disoriented. They both were. But it wasn't typically like her to no longer be able to find her way back home... The thought of it frightened her. She had no idea what to do.

"I'll be fine..." The young man then proceeded to cough a lot. Something was wrong with him. He was definitely hurt from his battle with the shadow wolf from earlier or whatever that was... Based on the recent wolf transformation that he recently went through, it would make a lot of sense for him to be sick. His body was changing because of whatever sickness he was suffering from, and this wasn't good at all.

"You don't look fine to me."

"You don't have to help me walk, you know?"

"I am not so sure about that. You're hurt, Michael." She reminded him.

"I don't care about that too much right now... The only thing I care about is what happened to us. We went out for a night hunt. We were attacked by wolves..."

"You saved me by jumping right in front of me and taking the bite of the wolf for me..." She interrupted him, getting reminded of what Michael did for her.

It was so kind of him to do that for her.

"Right..."

"But then you messed everything up and attacked me!" All of a sudden, Maleva switched her tone from kind and appreciative, to slightly angered and disappointed.

"I'm sorry. I shouldn't have done that. I don't know what came over me."

"It's okay now. You weren't yourself," Maleva looked away and blushed.

"But then... I transformed into this beast. You did too. We were also attacked by the wolves again. Things kept getting worse and worse. Things are still getting worse now. It's still not over. The worst thing that happened so far was this wolf that could walk on two feet and was made of shadows... What happened to it? Where did it go?" Michael was dying to know.

"You mean you actually don't know?"

"No... Why would I know...? I passed out and when I woke up, it was gone." He admitted to her.

"No. This isn't what truly happened, Michael..."

"What did then?"

She was still helping him walk around in the deep woods.

"Michael. You're the one who defeated it."

"I did what?" The young man was shocked to hear this news. He suddenly moved away from his childhood friend and moved on to his four. He nearly puked, but ultimately only ended up coughing a lot instead.

"Michael! Are you alright?"

"I'm fine... Ahn... Don't worry about me... Ugh..."

"Come this way. I believe I know where to go to make it back to the village."

"But I thought you said you didn't know earlier? You said that the woods no longer looked like they did before. You said that we were lost."

"And that was correct. I don't recognize these woods and no... We aren't lost. Not really..." Maleva totally refused to admit that they were lost.

"So, how do you know where to go?"

*Sniff! Sniff!*

Maleva could smell something pretty relevant.

"I wouldn't know how to explain it, but while I don't recognize these woods, I am somehow able to smell home. I know where to go."

"You're able to smell home? Wait a minute..."

*Sniff! Sniff!*

Michael tried as well.

"Are you kidding me? I can smell home too. I know where it is."

"Together we should be able to find our way back home. I just don't understand how we're able to smell something so far away like that."

"This has to do with what happened to us. We changed, Maleva. We are transforming into beasts. I felt like this ever since I was bitten, and you probably also felt like this ever since you were. Ever since I bit you," Michael theorized.

"Look, we'll try figuring out what happened to us when we finally are somewhere safe, okay?"

"Good idea. And speaking of which..."

Michael slowly stood back up.

It took a lot out of him, but he did it. He felt so worn out ever since the recent transformation.

"... I got something that is going to keep us safe..." Michael swiftly pulled something out of the holster on his right hip: His precious pistol. He hadn't been able to use it, ever since he was bitten and became sick. It was now time to use it again.

*Khump!*

Michael opened the barrel.

He took a look at how many bullets were left.

Two.

Only two.

"Two bullets aren't going to keep us safe for too long..."

*Shling!*

*Shling!*

Maleva swiftly pulled two of her daggers up.

"... My blades are."

*Cling!*

Michael closed the barrel.

He aimed at the woods. Practicing a bit.

But he couldn't see anything when looking from a far distance. His vision was all blurry. He couldn't aim, but he never mentioned it to Maleva. Something he should have done.

"Are you alright?"

"Yeah. I'm fine."

"Still want me to help you walk around?" She asked him.

"I never asked you to. I'm fine. I can walk by myself."

Michael stepped forward. He walked. More or less. He limped around quite a bit.

"If you say so."

"You coming?"

Maleva joined him. She followed him.

"So, I truly defeated the monster?" He asked her out of curiosity.

"You did, but you weren't yourself."

"What do you mean? I was changed? I had the wolf ears and the tail and claws and the fangs?"

"Not quite. It was a lot worse than that. You were a real wolf. Walking around on two feet," she finally admitted to him.

"You're kidding me?"

"I wish I was..."

He sighed in sheer desperation.

"Let's just find home again and then we'll worry about that."

*Sniff! Sniff! Sniff!*

"It's that way!" Michael pointed out after sniffing around.

# Chapter 9: Homecoming

"So, did I kill that monster after defeating it? I never saw its body after waking up."

"You didn't. It disappeared. It's still out there."

It was still deep into the night.

They were almost there. They were on the path that led to their home—to their village. They could smell it thanks to their new abilities that they had yet to understand.

"We're almost there!" Michael communicated to Maleva as the two of them were both running in the forest.

"I know!" Since she was running much faster than he was, she had to slow down for him at times. It didn't help that Maleva was much taller than Michael was. His legs simply couldn't keep up with hers, but at the same time, the young man did go through a lot. This complete transformation into a werewolf had taken a serious toll on him (understandably so) and he was recovering from it.

"We can make it!" Maleva attempted to cheer him up a bit.

"Oh, boy! I cannot wait to eat some warm stew from the inn! I'm so hungry!" Michael was jumping up and down with joy as he ran, following his busty childhood friend.

"Same!"

The two of them kept running until reality finally set in a bit.

Once again, it was quite important to remember that the monstrous beast, which had been after them from the beginning, was still out there...

As Michael and Maleva could both already smell some fresh stew being cooked, they suddenly heard a terrifying voice in the darkness...

"You truly thought that I was going to let you two get away like that?" It was the same dark and cold voice as the one of the shadow werewolves from earlier.

Michael and Maleva abruptly came to a brutal stop in the woods.

"You heard that?" The red-and-green-haired huntress asked Michael.

"Of course, I did."

"You'd really imagine that I would let one Moonlit Sin slip through my fingers?" The dark voice confronted them again. Yet, they couldn't see the wolf anywhere. They kept looking everywhere they could as they were both back-to-back, but they could never locate it.

*Oh no...* Maleva thought to herself.

"Moonlit Sin? What does it mean by that?"

"I really have no idea..." Maleva looked away, blushing. Obviously lying.

"Don't tell me you're still attempting to ignore that you are one of the Seven Deadly Moonlit Sins, sweet Maleva?" The dark voice tormented her.

"What? The Moonlit Sins? Just like the cursed people from the old legend?" Michael questioned Maleva.

"..." Maleva still wouldn't talk much.

"Do you mean that you never told your hunting partner about who you truly are?" The voice was always there, painfully whispering to the both of them.

"..." Maleva's head was down. She came across as shocked.

"You know what? It doesn't matter for now. We don't have to stand here and listen to this voice. Come on, Mal! We're going home!" Michael swiftly grabbed her by the hand and took her with him. They ran together in the direction of their village. They were almost there. They could smell how close it was. It was less than a kilometer away now for sure.

"Where do you think you're bringing my Moonlit Sin?" The dark and lustful voice asked him as he took her with him.

Michael and Maleva ran and ran as fast as they could until they couldn't anymore... Until they hit a wall!

"Ouch!" Michael was the only one who got hurt as he hit a semi-transparent barrier in the woods. They were stuck. They could no longer move forward anymore.

"What's that?" Michael asked.

"It's some kind of barrier..." Maleva investigated.

Then, before they knew it, a presence was felt behind them. It was the creature behind the dark voice.

They turned around and saw the same shadow werewolf as before but slightly different...

The werewolf came out from a wall of moldy trees and roots. The werewolf came across as if he was one with nature and his fur was made of leaves.

The werewolf slowly and silently preyed upon them as it moved closer and closer...

"I've waited so long to finally get my hands on a Moonlit Sin..." The beast was coming for them.

"Mal. Do you know anything about what they're talking about?" Michael asked her.

"Michael. I may not have been entirely honest with you," she admitted to him.

"What do you mean?"

"Don't you get it? She was never human to begin with!"

"That's true, Michael... I was born a Moonlit Sin..." She continued admitting to him.

"But I thought Moonlit Sins was a story that parents told their children before bed so they didn't venture too far in the woods at night?"

"That's also true, but the point is that people born with a Moonlit Sin inside of them are demons. *I am* a demon. Look. You didn't turn me into a werewolf when you attacked me the other day—I was already one."

"What are you talking about?" Michael couldn't believe what he just heard at first.

"It's the truth..." She mentioned.

"She's finally honest for once in her life. How cute?" The shadowy werewolf covered in leaves pointed out.

"So, you've been a wolf since when, Mal?" Michael had to know.

"Since... Forever..." She explained.

"Since birth?"

Maleva nodded. Not smiling at all.

"But since I've recently become a beast as well, does this mean that I am like you? I am a Moonlit Sin too?" The young man's mind was filled with all sorts of important questions.

"Oh? Do you believe you're like her? Forget about it, hunter-wannabe! She's the real deal! She's pure blood! You're just a prey that was in my way and was bit by one of my wolves and you're cursed because of it! The curse that has been bestowed upon you is more like a real sickness than a gift! You're trash! You're worthless! Just like a bastard! And I am going to kill you first before taking the Moonlit Sin for myself!" The vile night beast explained to the young man right before it began crawling their way. Processing and planning the next attack.

"No!"

Michael suddenly ran around Maleva and placed himself right in front of her. Standing there with his arms wide open.

"Michael?" Maleva didn't want him to get hurt by trying to protect her in any way, shape, or form.

"What do you think you're doing?" The werewolf roared at him.

"I am not going to let you hurt her! You're not leaving with her either!"

"Michael. You can't do this. Hide somewhere and let it take me."

"Never..." Michael was adamant about protecting her.

"You're making a mistake, Michael."

"That wouldn't be the first time that I do something, you tell me not to do it and that it turns out that you were right all along. Me hunting with you was one big mistake already, but I couldn't care less. I don't care if there's no way to defeat this monster. I just want to protect you with my life."

"Michael..." Maleva blushed. She had no idea what to say.

Meanwhile, the werewolf covered in leaves walked and then ran on two feet. Rushing toward them. Ready to strike them down.

"Your life is over, kid!" The beast coldly declared to him.

It was now and then that Michael remembered that he still had his weapon on him: His pistol.

*That's right! I still have two bullets left!*

He pulled his gun out. He looked into the barrel. Right. Exactly as he remembered it to be the case: Two bullets left in there.

"I will end you," the werewolf menacingly threatened him.

"Oh yeah?"

He quickly aimed at the beast.

His vision was still painfully blurry.

He still aimed and took his shot.

*Bang!*

Missed him...

The bullet went to his right between the trees.

"Michael?" Maleva was startled by the shot at first.

"You're weak," the werewolf analyzed him as he moved closer toward them.

*One more bullet... Here goes nothing...*

Michael aimed and took his shot at the beast again.

*Bang!*

He missed him again.

The bullet nearly touched him this time. It went right above his head.

His vision was even blurrier than before.

*No...* He thought to himself.

"Michael! We must get away!" Maleva was the voice of wisdom right about now.

"Too late..." The werewolf confirmed as it moved even closer and stole his weapon off of his hand and broke it by squeezing it in the palm of its hand!

The pistol fell into a million pieces everywhere on the ground. Scattered around.

"Michael. There might be one way to defeat it," Maleva thought of this at the last second.

"There is?"

# Chapter 10: Michael & Maleva

Still behind him, the young and busty woman gave him a reach around.

A reach around during that horrible and critical time? This didn't feel like something she should be doing right now. As she stood right behind him her soft chest comfortably rubbed against his back.

He could feel her nipples on his back. They were poking him. It was pleasant. It was quite pleasant, but this wasn't the time to do something like this. There was a werewolf standing right in front of them. Menacing their lives. Naturally, she wasn't only rubbing her tits in his back, she also had her right arm around him and she was reaching for his crotch.

Right about now, she was desperately attempting to pull his big young man's dick out of his pants. She had to.

"Mal, do you really think this is the right time to get kinky like that?" Michael finally confronted her and for a good reason.

"Do you trust me?" She whispered in his neck.

"Well apparently you have been a wolf your entire life and you never told me anything about that, so..."

"Ah... Good point... But can you just trust me now?"

"I cannot wait to acquire that Moonlit Sin!" the werewolf covered in leaves slowly stepped closer toward them. It was almost there. It was almost onto them.

He sighed.

"I guess I don't really have any other choice..."

"Good," Maleva nodded.

"What's your plan though? I truly hope it has nothing to do with you touching my crotch or something..." The young man couldn't stop blushing. His face had gone all red. He had absolutely no idea what she was trying to accomplish right about now.

"What? No. This is not what you think..."

Sure enough, this was what he thought it was...

Maleva wasn't reaching for his crotch—not really anyway, she had only slid the palm of her right hand over his crotch. Touching it a bit. Accidentally teasing and arousing him. No. What she was truly doing was that she reached for his hand.

"Huh?" There was a slight disappointment in his voice.

After reaching for his right hand, she opened it to give something to him. Something that she had been keeping in her left hand this entire time: It was a dagger. However it wasn't any dagger, it was one that was completely different from all the other ones he saw her use before.

This one was straight but had a sharp curve at the end of it. Almost like a scimitar, but it was a short blade, it was still a dagger. And there was something else that was definitely interesting—this blade was not of the same color as all the other weapons she used before. This one was silver. A pure metallic silver that shone brightly in the dark, even if the only thing that cast any light here in the shadowy woods was the moon itself. The handle of the weapon was of a crimson and leathery red color.

"What is this?" The scared young man swallowed the saliva he had accumulated in his mouth.

"It's a dagger. What does it look like, hmm?"

"Yeah I know that but it's different... It's silver."

"Take it."

"Why me? I've never used swords and daggers before. I'm not like you," he argued with her.

"Michael.. There's a reason why I haven't used this particular blade against the wolves and this ass-hole before. I am not supposed to use this weapon. I'm not even supposed to be holding it or be in its presence... Ahn..." Speaking appeared to be hurting her a lot. She gritted her teeth and desperately attempted to keep it together. What was happening to her?

"Are you hurt? What's going on?"

"I just told you: I'm not supposed to be holding this cursed thing. Take it! Take it from me!"

"Why?"

"Because it's made of pure silver and I'm a monster! I'm one of them! Take it! It shouldn't hurt you as bad as me since you're not pure blood!"

Michael finally agreed to take it from her.

*Schlink!*

The dagger made a certain sharp noise as he took it.

*So, is she saying that this is a good thing that I am not pure blood? I don't know what to think anymore...* Michael admitted to himself.

"Ohh..." Finally some relief for Maleva.

"What now?"

"Use it..."

"As if I'll allow you to do anything as such!" Then, before they knew it, the beast ultimately leaped into the air and launched its final attack on them. As it was mentioned before by it, the first one to go was definitely going to be the young boy. As soon as he's down, the beast would then be able to capture Maleva, also known as one of the Moonlit Sins.

"Michael!"

Holding the silver dagger for so long had her fall to her knees. She was defeated. She couldn't do anything more to help her childhood friend. The beast was coming! It pulled its right arm back and prepared to slash his throat with its claws.

*I am going to die... I am definitely going to die today...* This terrible, but realistic thought kept coming back to him over and over again.

Right before the werewolf covered in dead leaves could finally reach his position and slash his throat, he quickly moved his head back and took one final look at her... At Maleva...

Her eyes closed.

She was barely breathing anymore.

Michael bit his lower lip and turned his gaze back to the beast leaping toward him.

Then...

In a heartbeat...

Michael's facial expression switched from terrorized, to confident and determined. More determined than he ever was before in his life.

He swallowed the saliva that he had accumulated in his mouth again and finally held the silver dagger with both of his hands.

He raised the blade up!

Michael intended to slay the beast.

He pushed the dagger forward in the air and aimed for the beast's heart!

Now with the werewolf leaping in the air right above him, he never waited a moment longer and stabbed it as soon as possible!

However, who was going to complete the attack first? Him or it?

Only time was going to tell...

One second...

Another...

*Slash!*

Something happened!

Red blood was drawn.

What happened? There was so much chaos.

Michael's vision blurred again for a second. He had to close his eyes, diving into pure darkness before being able to re-open them again.

And when he did, he soon realized that the first one between the two to have completed their attack was the beast. It got him. He didn't.

The beast slashed his throat.

His throat was cut open.

It was too late.

Michael wasn't fast enough, yet, he was not going to let this 'little' problem change everything now. The beast slashing his throat was the perfect distraction he needed. Michael stood still and aimed the blade at its heart once more.

*Pook!*

He stabbed it!

Michael stabbed it right into the heart!

The werewolf covered in leaves roared in pain!

Then, everyone came down to the ground.

Crashing.

It was over.

Both of them were going to die tonight.

Including Michael.

Too bad for him he had such a short life.

At least he fell right next to Maleva and her big and perfectly soft breasts. His face accidentally fell right between them. The perfect place to die.

"Thank you for everything, Mal..." He whispered right before he shut his eyes.

# Chapter 11: The Drago

The next morning.

Michael woke up in a bed.

A real bed.

He wasn't lying down on grass anymore, but even more important than that, he was still alive somehow. Michael attempted to get up.

He wasn't able to at first, so he looked up. Looked around the room. Scanned it. He recognized this type of room. This was one of the few rooms there were at the local inn in the village.

The inn was called: 'The Drago'.

Formerly known as: 'The Slaughtered Lamb', but the name was changed when the place was sold a couple of years back.

The room he was in was quite simple. There was a single bed. One bedside table and a desk on the other side of the room. It was quite sunny. A yellow sunny light filled the room even though there was a curtain covering the window.

*I'm still alive? How is that the case?*

Michael attempted to get out of bed again.

He failed to do so, but he was able to sit up this time around.

Then everything came back to him...

*Maleva!*

The young man was finally able to get up. He jumped out of bed.

*Let's do a little recap here... What happened since I left the village to go on this hunt with Mal? I was able to kill a few dangerous wolves. I surprisingly had sex with Mal. A lot. I still feel it didn't happen and that it cannot be true, but it is. What else? Oh yeah! I was attacked by one of the wolves and the bite made me sick. It cursed me apparently. Then, we tried escaping and made it back to the village, but all of these wolves came together and made one giant werewolf... It nearly killed us, but... Oh... Yes. The dagger. The silver dagger I mean. Mal handed it to me and then I was able to stab it in the heart with it! But... Not before I was...*

Michael paused everything.

He remembered about the werewolf slashing his jugular and cutting it open.

He touched his throat.

There were a lot of bandages around his neck.

How did he survive this in the first place?

But that didn't matter anymore. He looked around the room again: No sign of Maleva. He had to find her. He crashed through the door and escaped.

***

*My life has been turned upside down. What matters the most to me now? Not changing into a wolf. Hoping I'll never change into a wolf again. Find Mal as soon as possible and then hope to spend as much time with her as I can. Try to live a normal life again!* Michael thought to himself as he ran down the corridor.

Originally, he thought about opening the doors of all the bedrooms in the hope of finding her, but then he realized and remembered that he now had a much better smell than he used to.

*Sniff! Sniff!*

Michael was able to smell Maleva's scent, which soon led him to one very specific room upstairs in the inn.

*She's that way!*

He rushed to that one room and aggressively opened the door as it turned out that it was thankfully unlocked.

He didn't find her in that room. The room was empty. No one was here. However, based on smell alone, Michael knew for a fact that she spent the night here. Same for him in his room. The bed was undone. She had recently woken up as well. He could tell.

*She was definitely here...*

***

Then, he followed her scent downstairs...

This was when he finally found her.

Maleva was adorably and beautifully sitting at one of the tables of the inn with her legs perfectly crossed together.

She was enjoying a cup of warm green tea, whose magnificent aroma filled the room and nearly entirely camouflaged her own scent. Thankfully not entirely, so Michael was able to locate her downstairs. Hot steam was coming out of the cup. Maleva was sitting with her back facing him. She did not see him at first.

However, she did hear his footsteps behind her. She probably smelled him as well, so she slowly turned around and laid her eyes on him for the first time this morning.

"Good morning, Michael," she greeted him with an adorable smile.

"Morning. What the hell is happening, Mal?" he immediately asked her after making his way up to her.

"It's breakfast," she announced to him, which was not the type of answer he was hoping for.

"Breakfast?"

"Come on. Come sit with me. I asked for tea for you," Michael noticed after the fact: There was a second cup of tea waiting for him on the table. However, there was more. Breakfast had already been served. Two plates could be seen on that table. The plates were covered in omelets and bacon and breakfast sausages and fruits such as pineapple slices, strawberries, and kiwis. This was a nice meal. Something that the both of them hadn't really had ever since this incident happened in the woods.

Maleva continued, "Breakfast is already served as well," She smiled at him as Michael felt more welcomed and appreciated now than he had ever been before in his life.

He, of course, accepted the offer and joined her.

He also noticed that Maleva's massive breasts were perfectly and comfortably sitting on the rim of the table. This made sense. There was no other way that this was going to work. Her tits were so large that they had to be resting on the side of the table like this.

It took Michael a lot to quit staring at her breasts. It requires a lot of bacon, to begin with.

"Thank you..." He soon thanked her as he shoved three slices of hot bacon in his mouth at the same time. Not thinking of the consequences that it was going to bring him since it was so hot.

"Don't mention it."

"Oh, it's hot! It's really hot!"

"What do you think it was going to be? Cold? The innkeeper just brought these plates to our table!" Maleva pointed out to him.

"So, what happened Mal? How did we get here? Who brought us here? I thought we both collapsed at the same time."

"Eat up and then I'll fill you in on the details. Okay?"

"Okay..."

More bacon entering Michael's mouth!

# Chapter 12: Cherrywood

After breakfast, Michael and Maleva took a walk outside.

It was finally daytime, which was a welcomed change of pace for the two of them since they both felt like they were stuck in this eternal night cycle during the recent hunt that, unfortunately, went so wrong.

"So, just to make sure I was not dreaming—werewolves are real?" Michael asked Maleva just to be a hundred percent sure. Naturally, he left The Drago Inn with a couple of bacon pieces in his hands, which he was munching on as they walked together around the modest and welcoming village.

"Werewolves are real."

"And you, my childhood friend, have been one since you were born?"

"That's right, and you're one as well now."

"Right. I still have to wrap my mind around that fact. From what I can remember, you were born a wolf because you're a pureblood, right?"

"You understood it all! Congratulations!" Maleva honestly clapped her hands for him. She was so happy and proud of him.

"And that makes me?"

"A cursed one," she declared.

"Oh great..." He sighed, "And we're both going to transform every full moon or what?"

"That's not exactly how that works. What you're talking about is more of a misconception..."

"A misconception?"

"It is true that all of us transform during the full moon, but this is not the only night we do. We can turn a lot more often than that. Pure-bloods can also resist transformations, but it is, unfortunately, rarely the case for bad-blooded-cursed-ones such as you," Maleva went on to explain to him.

"So, this means that I don't have any control over this shit?"

"No. I'm afraid you don't..."

"That's just great. Before I forget, I want to know what happened last night. We had collapsed on the ground. I thought the both of us were going to die. So, how did we end up back at the village and alive and well? Who brought us to the inn?" He desperately wanted to know.

"I did," she declared.

"You did?"

"I woke up not too long after you pierced the werewolf's heart and defeated it."

"Oh right! Speaking of that fucker!—"

"—It wasn't anywhere when I woke up. It was gone. So, I grabbed you in my arms and brought you back to the village myself. Thankfully the inn was still open when I arrived with you," Maleva swiftly interrupted him to tell him everything she knew.

"You were able to do all that on your own?"

"I guess so... Why?"

"..."

"Why?" She asked him again.

"You did so much. You saved my life countless times."

"You did too..." Maleva stopped him and attempted to make him realize that he also did the same thing for her.

"I'm not too sure about that. You did all the work," Michael shut his eyes and shoved another piece of steamy bacon in his mouth.

Then, as he munched on it, he spun around and re-opened his eyes to take one good look at the village that saw him get born...

"... Ah! *Cherrywood!* Our home!" Michael uttered as he raised both of his arms in the air. It felt great to be back home.

"Don't tell me—you're not leaving the village in a while, right?" She teased him.

"Ha-ha! You're right about that, Mal! You're sure right about that!"

Then, as the both of them were laughing and having fun, a dark presence was suddenly felt right behind them...

"Hey... What is that...?" Michael immediately sensed it.

"You felt it as well?" Maleva frowned.

The two nodded at the same time, and this was right before the two of them also spun around at the same time.

There was definitely something behind them...

After turning around, they both saw the same thing: There was an anomaly in the Cherrywood village.

It was a shadow.

A tall shadow that resembled the silhouette of a man. It was slowly going up a wall and it felt like it was staring right at them.

"It's the werewolf we fought while we were lost in the woods! I won't let it get away this time!" The brave, but quite headstrong young man immediately jumped to conclusions and rushed toward the shadow!

"No, Michael! Wait! Wait a second!" Maleva desperately attempted to stop him or slow him down at least, but she, unfortunately, wasn't fast enough.

"I've got you!" Michael was already up to the wall where the shadow was. The young man intended to punch the brick wall with his right fist. Why would he do something so stupid? It was too late. It had already done it.

*Boom!*

Michael punched the wall with all of his strength.

Dust everywhere.

There was now a hole in the brick wall.

The shadow was gone... Did he get it or did it get away before his strike?

In any case, Michael had to pull his fist out of that hole in the wall, but he was stuck in there.

He pulled once... No effect. He pulled twice... Still no effect. He pulled on his arm for the third time, but this time it worked! His arm finally came out of the hole he had made in the wall.

Although, there was only one little problem now... His right arm was no longer the same as it was before: His arm was covered in fur and he had claws for a hand. Michael recognized this... This was his werewolf arm!

Michael was still in his human form, but his right arm was now werewolf-like for some reason. Even if it wasn't night or a full moon or anything like that. What was going on?

"Mal? Did you see this?"

"Look out, Michael! Behind you!"

He barely had enough to turn around that the shadow, which attacked him earlier, was back for more. Attempting to surprise him.

It did.

The flying shadow rushed at him and hit him right in the face, cutting his left cheek.

*Slit!*

"Michael!"

However, what truly hurt the young man wasn't the cut at all. It was the fact that the shadow also accidentally made him drop the piece of bacon that was hanging out of his mouth that he still meant to finish.

The piece of delicious bacon then dramatically fell down to the ground in slow motion without Michael being able to rescue it in time.

"No!" Michael shouted!

It was too late.

The bacon strip had crashed in the grass down below...

Michael looked up at the shadowy shape in front of him and frowned.

"You did this..."

The next moment: Michael suddenly leapt toward the shadow creature and delivered a fatal blow to it—swinging his werewolf arm right at it!

"Ahhhh!"

The shadowy shape was instantly cut in half.

The shadow was no more.

What replaced it was a doll.

The shadow was gone, but a fractured doll sculpted in the shape of a wolf came down to the ground.

Rolling for a while before stopping...

When Maleva rejoined Michael, his werewolf arm was already gone and his human arm came back.

"Are you alright?"

"Yeah. I'm fine."

"The transformation was only partial and only lasted for a little bit it seems," she commented.

"Yeah. What was that shadow thing all about? What is that wolf doll?" the young man desperately wished to know.

"I'm not sure what it means yet."

Then. They both heard rambling. Folks heard this loud commotion involving the exterior wall of this house getting demolished. Pretty much everyone in the village heard this.

People were coming this way!

"We should probably not stick around," Michael mentioned.

"You're right. Let's go!"

Maleva kindly placed her arm around his shoulder as they left.

"Let's go somewhere calmer..." she tried reassuring him.

They then both left in a hurry.

The strange wolf doll soon subtly and slowly moved by itself after they left. Bobbing from left to right.

# Chapter 13: Somewhere Calmer

"It shows that you were my childhood friend and that we haven't spoken in years up until recently..."

Michael and Maleva came back to the inn.

"How so? What do you mean?" Maleva asked him as she curled up with him in bed. This was upstairs in The Drago Inn and the room they were in was Maleva's. Their rooms had only been rented for one night, so they technically had no right to be here anymore. Additionally, a maid was bound to come in at any time now to clean up the place and prepare the room for the next people who were going to rent it.

They were definitely playing with fire and they were soon about to run out of time.

Michael was lying down on his back in bed while Maleva was over him, semi-hovering on top of him with her arms on both sides of him. Their faces were so romantically close to one another that their noses nearly touched.

"*Michael* was the name that was written inside of the fur coat that was serving as a blanket when I was left as a baby in Cherrywood.

It's the name that was given to me by the people who dumped me here. But I always felt like it wasn't my name."

"So, where is this going? You don't want me to call you Micahel anymore, even though this is what I've been calling you ever since we were little?" She possessed this tongue-in-cheek facial expression about her at the moment almost as if she somehow found him quite funny.

"You could just call me by my last name then."

"Your last name?" she cocked her head to the side.

"Do you remember what it is?"

"*Redheart*—the name of the type of tree that they found you at the base of. I remember now."

"I had no idea you'd remember something like that..."

"I do. So, just to be clear, do you want me to call you *'Redheart'* instead of *'Michael'*? It doesn't make any sense to me," she argued with him.

"Honestly? I don't care."

"Um... How about we talk more about it a bit later, huh? For now, I just want to soak up the moment while I have you for myself all alone," She pressed her big tits tighter against his chest as she hovered above him.

"B-but Mal... You clearly had me for you all alone ever since I stupidly followed you on that hunting evening..."

She scratched her head for a bit. Thought about this for a while as she remembered just how much to herself she had him in the past couple of days.

Michael was right.

"Guess you're right but that wasn't quite enough for me. I need more of you, Michael. And now that you know what I am, I'm sure you'll understand why I need it so much..."

"You're referring to the fact that you're one of the Moonlit Sins, right?"

"Right. But not only any of the sins—I am lust."

*How could I forget? It completely slipped out of my mind with the werewolf attack as we were trying to make it back home. That's right! She's lust! So, does that mean that she always wants to have sex or something like that?* The thought of it gave the young man an even bigger erection. Maleva easily felt his throbbing manhood against her belly as she was still on top of him.

"I am *your* lust," Maleva added before she kissed him right on the lips. She couldn't resist him anymore. The boy became harder during that kiss, however, it was nothing compared to when she pushed her long and erotic tongue inside his mouth. Their kiss continued and evolved with their tongues, which resulted in him becoming absolutely rock solid. His young boy's cock was aching to come out of his pants. Something that she was definitely going to help him out with.

Uncontrollably aroused, she slid down in the hope to get at the level of his waist. She soon pulled down on his pants and then also pushed down on his underwear to take his dick out of the inside of his boxers, which naturally bobbed out of there.

Maleva didn't even bother to caress or stroke his penis or anything like that, she simply dashed right ahead and had it enter her mouth! The next second: She was sucking on his hard dick. Blushing with her eyes shut. Enjoying herself.

"Mal. It's pretty late in the morning now. The maid is bound to come up here any second. Someone's going to catch us."

She stopped sucking on his cock.

"Then, do you want me to stop?" she offered to him as she pulled her large breasts out of her top and erotically peeled the paw-shaped nipple covers off of her tits. The fishnet top was still on, but her boobs had fully been unleashed on him.

"Your tits..."

"Do you want me to put them away, then?"

"No... Please, no..."

"I'm just kidding," she smiled, "Do you want to have some fun with them? Like *this?*" she added as she delicately grabbed his cock and properly placed the tip of it, so it would go between her udders. Then, the young man firmly pushed his member as deep as it would go, so he could fuck her breasts.

"My dick just disappeared between your breasts..."

"As it should be the case," she comforted him.

Then, the fun began...

Michael quickly became so excited that he pushed his dick even deeper between her breasts and erotically proceeded to move his member back and forth in order to have sex with her chest!

The arousal was so great for him that he began producing a relatively healthy and thick amount of pre-cum in no time until he was brought closer and closer to a fast point of ejaculation.

The young man was eventually going to cum sooner rather than later and with his childhood friend, Malva now holding on to her tits and softly squishing them on both sides of his rod, it was perfectly understandable that he was going to cum sooner rather than later. Definitely a lot sooner than he could ever foresee it.

"I'm cumming! I already have to cum, Mal!"

"It's okay! Let it all out, Michael! You can even cum between them, Michael *Redheart!*" Maleva teased him by offering him to cum between her tits and by also calling him by his full name.

*Splat!*

Michael ejaculated right away between her udders!

Satisfaction. From both sides. They were so happy and relieved.

"How do you feel?" she sweetly whispered.

"Mal…" out of breath, the only thing he felt like he could say was her name. That was the only thing that mattered to him: Her name.

"We should probably get out of here now though," she admitted right at the exact same time the door opened!

Oh, no! The door just opened!

They hadn't taken the time to lock it first.

The both of them turned to the door.

"The door…" Michael knew something like this was going to happen.

"Too late I guess…" Maleva whispered.

However, the person who opened the door and came inside was not the maid. Bloody hell! It wasn't even a person. It was something else—instead of being a person, it was a wolf doll. The same wolf doll they briefly saw on the ground earlier after Michael cut down this shadow creature in half.

The wolf doll *never* moved.

It only stumbled and rolled inside the bedroom after the door was opened, but who did this? Who opened the door? To be honest, it never even truly felt like the door was ever opened in the first place. The door was definitely ajar. Cracked open. But it never felt like the doll entered the room. It felt more like it had always been there, to begin with, but that none of them ever noticed it in the room before.

To be clear: The doll was *not* animated.

"The doll from earlier?" Maleva was oddly shocked.

"Now, I have to inspect this doll!" Michael already jumped out of bed! Ready to take action!

# Chapter 14: Lycanna

The tiny wolf doll was brought outside.

Since they couldn't stay any longer inside of the bedrooms at The Drago since they had only rented them for one night and one night only (them having only enough of a budget big enough to get them one night), they had no other choice but to leave before the dreaded maid showed up.

Naturally, they didn't go in the direction of where they were attacked by the shadow wolf. They instead took a walk in another direction in the village.

"It's too bad we don't have places of our own in Cherrywood..." Michael argued.

"Right. Come to think of it: Where do you live now, Michael?" She was pretty curious to know.

"Same place as it has always been the case..."

"The foster home?" she remembered that this used to be the place a long time ago.

"Yep. They still keep me there because there is one tiny spare room for me and because I helped out doing a lot of the cooking there. However, I'm surprised *you*, of all people, don't have an apartment or a house of your own at this point. After all, you're the best hunter we have in town and you always bring the most food to people as well as kill the most dangerous animals that are roaming around the village. How can you not afford a home at this point?" the young man desperately wanted to know.

"I don't hunt for money. I *never* did. I hunt for everyone to have food. I never asked for any money for what I hunt. I never want anyone to starve. Also, protecting Cherrywood only makes sense. Besides, I don't need a home. I categorically prefer camping in the woods. Last night, I went to the inn for rooms because we were in pretty bad shape. That was the only reason, really. Well, that and the fact that you are not used to camping at all, but that's beside the point..."

"It takes a wild girl who wants to camp in the middle of the woods almost every night. I respect that," Michael blushed and looked the other way. What was going on? Why was he feeling so shy with her all of a sudden that he needed to turn his head away from her for a second?

In reaction to him doing so, she did it as well. She blushed and then looked away...

The both of them remained silent for a few seconds as they continued walking in the middle of the village...

As the two of them were no longer saying a single word to one another, Michael looked around and realized that a lot of people were randomly staring at them. He had no idea why, but it was the case.

People were talking amongst themselves about them while staring at them. Whispering.

Then, on her side, Maleva also noticed the exact same thing at the exact same time. People staring at them and whispering.

What were they saying?

Well, they were all whispering amongst each other, but thankfully, since Michael and Maleva were both wolves now, they could hear much better than a human would. This was nothing new for Maleva since she had always been a wolf due to the fact that was born like this as a Moonlit Sin, but this was completely new to Michael.

"They left town for a couple of days and now that they are back, they're some kind of couple now? What is this?" one elderly woman whispered to her friend. Michael heard everything she said.

"Maleva is our huntress and she's an adult. What about him, huh? Isn't he a young boy or something?" her friend replied to her. Michael continued listening to their conversation.

"No, he's way older than that. He's the same age as her. He just looks much younger and is much shorter than her. Still looks disgusting and wrong that the two of them are together now for some reason," A different woman came in and joined their little discussion in the street. Michael couldn't shut it off. He was forced to hear everything they said about them.

"What's happening, Mal? They're saying that we're a couple. As well as a bunch of other things..." Michael finally broke the silence and spoke to her again.

"You can hear them too?" she came across as surprised.

"Yeah. Of course, I can."

"Then, this means that you're getting used to your new wolf senses already. Um... Don't worry about what they're saying. Try to ignore them..."

"That is going to be difficult..." he admitted to her.

"Just try. Okay?"

"Anyway... So, you still have it?" Michael then remembered that they had something to do.

"Yes, of course," she replied right after clearing her throat, "Let's go this way so no one bothers us too much," Maleva pointed at one alleyway between two houses.

"Not a bad idea..." he followed her into the alleyway and almost as soon as they turned the corner, Maleva slid her right hand into her cleavage and searched for something in there.

"What are you doing?" Michael grew deeply confused by what she was doing.

"I'm pulling it out..."

"You what?"

*Thump!*

She did it!

She pulled the tiny wolf doll from earlier from between her big and perfectly soft tits!

"You placed it in there while I wasn't looking?"

"Right..."

"Why?"

"What? Don't look at me like that, I didn't have a bag on me."

She held the doll in her hands and held it high.

"Now... Let's examine this thing. I suspected it to be something awful earlier, but now I am certain that this doll is bad news. It probably contains the same dark power as the entity that recently attacked us in the woods," Tired of waiting for this doll to do something, she suddenly began hitting it with her fists. She was *this* much closer to bashing it against a wall! Maleva had no patience for this sort of thing.

"Hey! Wait up! What are you doing?"

"Trying to wake it up or opening it if I have to..."

"Hold on! We have no idea what this thing is! You're going to break it for no good reason!"

Then, out of care for this interesting artifact, Michael tried rescuing it from her hands and grabbed it from her. Stealing it from her. However, as soon as the young man made physical contact with the doll, it suddenly began changing form!

The wolf doll woke up as Maleva alluded to earlier.

It changed from a doll to some kind of small animal: A baby-looking humanoid wolf!

"What the?" Maleva had never seen anything quite like this before.

"What's this?" Michael even less so.

The animal opened his eyes and looked straight at Michael.

It smiled at him right after yawning.

"My name is *Lycanna!* Nice to meet you!"

# Chapter 15: Loupmignon

This was an emergency!

No one could see this... thing, so Michael and Maleva brought it out of Cherrywood as soon as possible!

"What the hell are you?" Michael questioned the small beast that he still held in his hands. Thankfully, there was no way that anyone was going to see this tiny and speaking wolf on the outskirts of town here. It was only Michael, Maleva, and this little thing here...

"For the last time: My name is Lycanna!" she cried out with the most adorable and soft girl's voice in the world.

"We got that already. I believe he meant: *What are you?*—What is your species? We never saw a tiny wolf, who could talk before," Maleva pointed to her.

"What? You two never met a *loupmignon* before?"

"A what?" Michael nearly dropped the damn thing after hearing this strange word.

"Hey, hey! Careful! Don't drop me! A loupmignon! Never heard of it?"

"I never did..." Maleva frowned as she personally felt she should know what the hell this was all about.

"A loupmignon is a spirit wolf damn it!" she declared.

"A spirit wolf? Do you actually mean?" This piqued Maleva's interest. Almost as if she knew some of what she was talking about.

"Mal? You know something about this?" Michael turned to her.

"It's impossible..." she murmured.

"No, it's not! Now, let me down! Let me down!" the small animal was absolutely out of control!

"No way!" Michael wouldn't do something like that.

"Mike. Put her down," Maleva gave him one serious look.

"Why the hell would I do something like that? So, it runs away or something?"

"Put her down, now!"

"Give me one good reason, then!" Michael didn't want to listen to her.

"I believe that this tiny and speaking animal is here to serve you!" Maleva finally let loose and shouted at the young man!

"Um... What? What did you just say?" he stopped her right away.

"Finally some good sense!" the loupmignon yawned and smiled in relief. She smiled a bit as well.

"Okay, then... Whatever..." Michael finally agreed to put her back down on the ground after holding her in his hands for so long... Lycanna, the loupmignon, who was a minuscule humanoid wolf of about two feet tall was more than glad to be let go. The wolf spirit with the tiny body, short legs, and arms was finally freed again. While the rest of her body was pretty small, she had a big rounded head and two large blood orange eyes. Her fur was dark brown with a few white stripes. A pair of fangs was hanging out of her mouth at all times. She was adorable.

Lycanna wore a blood-orange tunic and a cute skirt.

"Thank you," Maleva was glad he listened to her.

"Thanks a lot my boy," even Lycanna thanked him.

"So, you're supposed to serve me or something like that? I don't need a talking wolf to help me with anything, you know?" the young man confronted the loupmignon who towered over her.

"That's where you're wrong! You need me in order to defeat the big, bad wolf that is lurking around town!" Lycanna declared.

"What? You know about that?" Michael questioned her.

"Guys... We need to go and continue this conversation elsewhere... Someone's coming this way..." Maleva whispered to them as she managed to detect someone approaching on the road. Her huntress skills came in pretty helpful again.

She was right! A woman was coming this way!

"Let's go..." Michael was already on the move.

Michael swiftly picked Lycanna up again and they all left as soon as possible.

"Hey! What are you doing? Put me down! Put me down!

Same old thing.

***

Besides the fact that they both felt like they should hide the wolf spirit from the rest of town, it also felt right to them to escape Cherrywood for a while for other reasons. Escaping the judgmental stares and murmurs of the people in town was immensely appreciated. All these bad looks only because they were seeing them together... It was so strange. They definitely had to get to the bottom of that, but, unfortunately, now was not the right time to do so.

So, they left Cherrywood for now and soon arrived at some kind of abandoned farm up on the hills.

"What is this place, Mal?" Michael questioned her upon arriving there.

"Remember when I told you that I liked camping a lot?" Maleva smirked.

"Yeah? What about it?"

"Well, the woods aren't the only place where I like to go camping... This is my secret place—the Ruby Farm!" She welcomed Michael and Lycanna to this run-down farm that had countless beautiful trees with ruby-red leaves.

"The Ruby Red farm? What is this place, really?" Michael wondered.

"Oh! Sweet! So, is this the place you two are going to fall in love at?" the wolf spirit inappropriately asked the two of them.

"Fall in love?" Michael was absolutely shocked to hear this coming out of the loupmignon's mouth.

"Um... Well..." Meanwhile, Maleva was feeling all weird about this. She looked the other way. Avoiding looking at Michael. Sweat Drops appeared all over the back of her head. She was acting weird.

"Okay, then! But are you at least going to have sex here?" Then, it was at that moment that Lycanna shouted something even more inappropriate than the last thing she said.

"What's wrong with you?" Michael snapped at her and attempted to run after her. Probably in the hope of picking her up from the ground again and shaking her a bit. Unfortunately, for him, the wolf spirit was a tad bit faster than he was.

"What do you think you're doing? Come on, Michael! Stop running after me like that!"

"Having sex here...?" Maleva whispered to herself, still acting all shy and weird.

"I bet this is what she wants the most right now!" the wolf spirit pointed out as she continued escaping Michael.

"You are not making any sense!"

"No! She's right!" Maleva finally spun back around.

Everything stopped!

Everyone did.

Michael and Lycanna both stopped moving.

"Um?" Michael wasn't too sure what was going on.

"See? Told you?" the loupmignon blew him a raspberry.

"She's right! I want to have sex with you again, Michael! Earlier, I was pleased to pleasure you at the inn, but I need more now! I can't wait anymore!" Maleva's body was overheating. She was sweating a lot. Blushing. Her skin had turned all red.

Maleva, the lust sin was lusting for him...

# Chapter 16: The Farm

It was nighttime before they knew it.

While it was clearly not a full moon tonight, there was still a bright and oppressive crescent moon in the dark sky that cast an orange-red light on the farm.

It wasn't only a full moon that could have an effect on wild beasts such as wolves. Any phase or form of the moon possessed a strange effect that could be felt by both the purebloods and the ones who were cursed.

Michael, Maleva, and Lycanna all found refuge in the house on the farm. Lycanna, who more or less behaved like a young kid up to this point, was left alone in the living room downstairs. Barely a couple of seconds after crashing on the old couch, and she was already snoring.

*Zzzzzz....*

So, the two others then took the only room with a bed in it and that was upstairs.

Finally, alone, Maleva wasted no time tackling the young man onto the bed and moved on top of him! Similar to how it happened in that room of The Drago earlier today.

"Ahn!" Michael was surprised by her pushing him onto the bed at first.

*I know exactly what she wants and I can't blame her... She pleasured me earlier at the inn, but she didn't get anything out of it, really. I know she takes a lot of pleasure out of pleasuring me, but still... Too bad we didn't have time to do more earlier at The Drago because I totally would have...* Michael thought as he observed his busty childhood friend going on top of him.

"The wolf spirit was right earlier: I want to have sex with you!" she lustfully announced.

"I had that feeling..."

Maleva turned her head and looked through the cracked window in the room. She saw the crescent moon up in the dark sky. She smiled.

"I don't only want to have sex with you again—I also want to go deeper with it," she admitted to him.

"Which means?" The young man was still pretty oblivious and innocent to some of that stuff if he was being honest.

"I want you to cum inside of me more..." she revealed to him. This was something that they had done before, but never repeated too much. So, did this mean that she was into this kind of stuff? She liked cream–pies? She truly did?

In direct reaction to what she asked of him, his lovely cock suddenly began twitching! Maleva felt it.

Then, one thing led to another and the huntress went ahead and pulled his pants and underwear down in order to reveal just what was twitching so much in there...

Totally accidentally—his meat went slapping on the side of her face, all over her left cheek. Cock-slapping her!

"Ara... Ara...." This had the effect of amusing her more than anything. She didn't mind it at all, "Looks like you're also into this idea..."

He was.

Maleva wasted no more time and climbed on top of his cock without even taking the time to fully undress the young man. Only need his dick. The tip of his glans rubbed against her slippery vaginal lips until she had him enter inside of her in no time.

Before he knew it, she was jumping on top of his cock as he was fucking her as if it had been an eternity since the last time the two ever had sex together like this. In reality, it had only been a couple of days during the failed hunting trip.

"Yes! Yes! Your cock feels so good! It feels amazing! I'm heating up! I feel like something is changing inside of me!" she moaned as she bounced up and down on top of his dick. She was right. Something was indeed changing inside of her. She *was* changing. The crescent moon in the dark sky definitely had a powerful effect on her. To the point of slowly transforming her into a wolf girl during the sexual act.

"Aww.... Ohhh! Yes!"

Then, her moaning slowly turned darker and darker until it shifted into a howling—a wolf howling!

This was bound to wake up the little one downstairs.

As soon as the first howling session was done with, Maleva had changed to the point of gaining her wolf ears, irises, fangs, claws, and tailback!

However, there was something else that happened tonight during this wolf transformation: In addition to all the classic werewolf trademarks that she gained during the transformation, Maleva's body also changed in another way. Her bust size increased! Her chest became bigger after she became a wolf! She gained a size or two and the shape of her breasts slightly became a bit more like real melons.

*She not only changed into a wolf this time, but her breasts also became bigger! How does that work?*

"Mal..."

"I know I've turned into a werewolf again..."

"No... Mal... Your tits..."

"My breasts? Oh, yeah, this kind of thing often happens when I'm in heat..."

She had successfully transformed into her werewolf form during sex and this was all to Michael's merits to be honest, since she truly needed to be heated up and turned on for this to happen. Especially when it wasn't a full moon. This was significant. A werewolf girl needed to be in heat to be turned into her werewolf form and this was exactly what was happening here.

However, Maleva wasn't too hard to be brought to this sexual heat state since she was not only one of the Moonlit Sins, but she was indeed Lust out of all of them. So, if Lust found someone she was attracted to and turned on by, she was definitely going to be in heat a lot. Turned out that Maleva AKA Lust had indeed found someone she was attracted to a lot and that person was no other than Michael himself.

"Aw! I'm coming! I'm coming, Michael!"

*She's coming? This seems pretty serious...*

"I'm coming so much! Yes! Aw!"

However, then she proceeded to...

"Oowwwwll!" Maleva howled at the moon again at the same time that she came! Furthermore, it validated the fact that she probably woke Lycanna who was simply downstairs because of this remarkably loud howl.

*I'm cumming as well...*

"I have to cum, Mal..."

"Perfect! Then, please cum inside of me, Michel! I want you to fill me up real good, so I have little Redheart babies growing inside of me!" she begged him to do so.

Well, this was no longer a matter of choice now since the young man had to cum now and couldn't hold on anymore.

*Fwip! Fwip! Fwip!*

Michael swiftly ejaculated inside of her and filled her up as she just demanded it. With her being in heat as much as she was, there was a high amount of chance that he was going to impregnate her with this massive load.

"Your load! It's so big! I can feel it inside of me... Thank you, Michael... Thank you..." she was still moaning...

The breeding process could finally begin!

# Chapter 17: Bark In The Barn

The next day, Michael, Maleva, and the wolf spirit Lycanna spent lots of time together. Most of the day in fact.

Maleva showed them the entire farm.

***

By the time it was evening, Lycanna had gone her separate way and she went to explore the croplands on her own without the others.

So, Lycanna was off to do her own things?

This meant that this would allow some free and private time for the two lovers, Michael and Maleva.

"I know exactly what to do now..." she sensually whispered into his ear as she pulled him inside the old barn.

"Huh? What is that supposed to mean?"

"You'll see!" Maleva brought him into the barn and made certain to shut the door behind them.

*Thud!*

The fall wasn't too bad since the young man landed right on top of a soft pile of hay!

Maleva towered over him.

"What's wrong?" he questioned her as he definitely noticed that something was wrong with her. She intentionally squeezed the side of her big tits with her arms to make them collide with one another. Making them look even bigger than they already were. She gazed at the pretty boy in front of her.

"I'm still in heat," she confirmed to him.

"You are?"

"And even though you came inside of me last night, I want to make sure I'll be pregnant with your babies, so please take me in this barn," she begged her mate to do this to her.

"How are you still in heat?" Michael was still hung up on that. Who could blame him after all?

Unable to resist him and his charms anymore, Maleva fell for him once more and joined him in the pile of hay!

Still enthralled with the breeding aspect of their relationship and the fact that she desperately wished to be impregnated by Michael, she soon found her way between his legs and undressed the young man! She pulled his pants and his underwear down to finally reveal his big cock! She had been craving it all day! Since his member was already extremely wet and his head covered in thick pre-cum, she decided to go at it pretty raw and not do anything to him before climbing on top of his cock and having some rough sex with him!

However, there was only one little thing she hadn't thought of ahead of time: It was almost night. It was dark outside. The crescent moon in the sky cast a harsh blood-orange light on them both, which entered through a series of opened windows on the side of the old barn.

This time, it was Michael out of both of them who was affected by the moonlight the most. Maleva stayed in her human form at the moment while the young man soon transformed into the beast that he had recently become!

At the same time that he turned into a wolf boy, he became a lot more aggressive and picked Maleva up. Seizing all control of her! After grabbing her, he spun her around in the pile of hay and pushed his huge and beautiful wolf cock against her wet pussy lips!

"Aww! So aggressive! I like that!"

Even though she could be a pretty dominant young woman at times, she sure enjoyed being dominated herself. The wolf boy rigidly moved her around and placed her in a doggie-style pose. The most appropriate pose for this sort of sexual performance. Before they knew it, the wolf boy progressively morphed into a complete werewolf. He was so aroused and the power of the crescent moon was so strong that he couldn't resist.

"Ooouwwwll!" he howled at the moon as he pushed his cock much deeper inside of her pussy, making love to her!

"Ahn! I'm coming! Yes! You're fucking me too hard! I'm coming! I'm coming! Mhn!"

Maleva was not the only one who had vowed to come inside the barn. The same thing was also happening to Michael, the bad-blood werewolf.

So aroused by his woman as he banged her like a werewolf, he ejaculated inside of her without being able to hold anything back!

"Owwnnnwn!" he howled one more time as he filled her pussy up. Exactly as she wished for him to do to her.

A mere few seconds later, Maleva was completely filled with his biggest load to date!

However, even though she was so filled up that it was normally going to be dripping out of her—overflowing out of her, there was something naturally set in motion to prevent this from ever happening: The werewolf quickly spun around while still being inside of her, continuing to fuck her as powerfully as he could. Now, the two of them were back-to-back. His wolf cock was still deep inside of her.

Michael had knotted her.

None of his load could ever come out of her for as long as they would be like that.

Still massively erect, the werewolf never stopped penetrating her. Having his way with her.

Michael even went as far as barking in the barn as he made love to her and her sweet and tight pussy.

"I can feel your load inside of me... It's even bigger than last night..." she admitted to him, even though he already knew that.

Back-to-back fucking like this could look pretty silly from an outsider's point of view, but this was actually as primal and vicious and animalistic as it could become. Nothing was silly here for the two of them. They enjoyed every last second of it.

This outsider's point of view was no other than the wolf spirit girl herself, Lycanna.

She showed up!

Unbeknownst to them, she still showed up.

She hid on the wooden railing of the second floor of the barn. Looking down at all the action. Enjoying the view from up there.

"Looks like you knotted her real good!" Lycanna observed.

They had no idea she was up there.

Maleva had been impregnated by Michael.

It was different this time. This time, this truly worked as he knotted her for the first time. Therefore, preventing any cum from dripping out of her pussy.

He successfully bred her.

Since she was going to be pregnant because of him—which was already the case, she was already pregnant—her body automatically reacted to this drastic change and her breasts became much heavier. Bigger as well as it was the case last night during the momentary breast expansion. With her chest becoming larger and heavier, they also became slightly more low-hanging.

This was to be expected as milk production had finally been activated in her body and her breasts were getting filled up with it.

She felt it in her tits.

"Oh! Michael, you bred me for sure because I'm feeling my tits getting filled up with milk!—" Naturally, before she could even finish her sentence, milk started to squirt out of her boobs!

"Ahn!" she moaned out loud as it happened.

Lactation production was in full swing!

Then, at the same time, back on the second floor of the barn, Lycanna received a nightly visit.

A dark shadow appeared behind her.

Crawling its way up in the back of the wolf spirit.

# Chapter 18: Mating & Breeding

It was time to get back to Cherrywood.

When Michael, Maleva, and Lycanna arrived there, it was pretty early in the morning. The sky was of beautiful pink color. No one was outside since it was so early, but the three of them all felt a negative energy roaming around town

*Sniff! Sniff!*

Michael analyzed the area with his bestial smell.

*Sniff! Sniff!*

*Sniff! Sniff!*

Maleva and Lycanna both did the same, but Michael beat them to it.

"Is that the presence you smelled and felt earlier in the barn?" Michael asked the wolf spirit.

"It is! Same thing!" the short wolf girl immediately recognized it!

"I still can't believe you were peeping on us back there in the barn..." Maleva was so mad. She folded her arms together and blushed, looking back at everything they did back at the farm and now knowing that Lycanna was probably watching everything like a total pervert. It wasn't for no good reason that Lycanna now had a big bump on the top of her head. She deserved it!

"What do you want me to say? You two make for a great couple already!" the wolf spirit voiced her opinion out loud.

"We are not really a couple, you know....?" Maleva blushed even more as she had no idea if it was right to even say something like that in the first place.

"Silence! Someone's approaching..." Michael stopped everyone. Danger was incoming!

He was right because before he could truly have enough time to place himself between the enemy and Maleva and Lycanna, it was mostly already too late, but Michael still felt like he could make it in time. He wasn't about to give up on saving them anything soon.

A pair of tall shadows rushed to them not too far from the entrance of town!

Lycanna was the sole target here.

The two shadows nearly had her, but Michael thankfully moved fast enough!

"Aaaahhhh!" Michael was already enraged at that point as he didn't want to see any of these two girls getting hurt in any way.

Similar to how it happened last time, Michael swiftly and partially transformed into the cursed beast that he now was!

His right arm turned into a furry one and much more muscular! His hand was replaced by claws!

"Ahhh!" Michael screamed one more time as he attacked the two shadows!

Saving Lycanna just in time, beast Michael slashed the two tall shadows and stopped them both right before it was too late!

The shadows quickly faded and then they burst into pink flames!

The two enemies were gone. Almost as if they had never existed.

"You two alright?" he asked them as he stood there, out of breath.

"I'm fine..." Maleva mentioned.

"Y-you... You saved me?" Lycanna, the short girl looked up at Michael with pink hearts in her eyes. She was falling in love with the young boy. She now saw him in a different light.

"Are you sure you're alright, Lycanna?" he raised one eyebrow as his werewolf arm soon faded back into his regular human arm.

"Looks like these same forces Lycanna felt back at the barn have already come to town." This was exactly what Maleva originally feared.

"Let's hope there isn't more. Lycanna," Michael turned back to her, "Do you know anything about these shadows?" he asked her.

"You-you saved me..." the short wolf girl was still blushing with big, pink hearts in her eyes.

"Uh. Forget about it..." Michael wasn't going to get anything out of her now as she, unfortunately, wasn't herself.

The young man turned back to Maleva, finally giving up on the wolf spirit.

"—."

When he turned back to the huntress, he suddenly noticed for the first time since leaving the old farm that Maleva's breasts were much bigger and heavier-looking than they were before he bred her in the farmhouse and in the barn. This wasn't only some momentarily breast expansion that had been caused by the recent werewolf transformation, this was something else. This was some natural breast expansion because of the fact that she was now a pregnant woman.

The young boy didn't say anything when he noticed her bigger tits, but he definitely blushed a lot. Feeling hotter.

Embarrassed. Deeply aroused. His cock throbbing in his pants. He had no idea what to do at this point.

Maleva did notice him staring at her chest and blushing though.

"What's wrong, Michael?"

"Nothing…" he swiftly looked the other way!

"I'm falling in love with Michael!" he could hear Lycanna whispering behind his back, which prompted him to sigh pretty loudly.

***

Later, but still pretty early in the morning as the sky was still reddish-pink.

Michael, Maleva, and Lycanna all sneaked into the foster home where the young man lived or used to inhabit before the hunting incident happened recently. The few people there were still deep asleep since it was so early.

Michael brought Maleva into his bedroom and they left Lycana in the dining room so she could have a snack. Michael ended up giving the short wolf girl a snack. In this case, he gave her a nice, big bowl of cereal drowning in cold milk. Lycanna was so adorable as she sat on a massively large bench at the dining table. Her feet playfully swung in the air since she was too short to touch the floor.

So, it was at that moment that Michael seized this opportunity to sneak behind her back and to take Maleva into his old room...

He had the newly pregnant woman come onto his bed.

Pretty exhausted from their trip, she laid down on the side of her body in the bed and Michael went around her and lay down with her. Even though she was deeply tired, Maleva knew exactly what her boy wished for her. And Maleva wouldn't be the living embodiment of Lust if she didn't want to have sex over and over again. Because this was totally what she was craving once more even if they had plenty of sex back at the farm.

Her orange thong hadn't been removed yet. Realistically knowing what the young man desired out of her, she quickly pulled her thong out of the way, so he could insert his hard cock inside of her without having to remove her underwear.

"There you go, you come in..."

She let him inside of her.

*Plop!*

He was inside her!

Michael was fucking a lovely, pregnant woman!

"Quick... We don't have much time before Lycanna finishes her bowl of cereal..." she lustfully reminded him as he had already made her moan a lot!

# Chapter 19: A Pregnant Wolf

Judgmental looks!

The townspeople all noticed her pronounced pregnant belly as they walked in the streets of Cherrywood.

"They're all staring at me..." Maleva murmured to Michael.

"No, they're not."

The young boy looked around to see if there was any truth to what she was talking about even though he just said that this wasn't the case. However, when Michael took a look around, he realized that she was absolutely right. All these neighbors watched them as they walked in the streets.

Why were they staring at them so much?

Why were they staring at *her* so much? What did she do?

"Okay... Maybe they're staring a bit..." Michael admitted.

"Told you. Now, I can't tell if they're staring at my enlarged breasts or at my pregnant belly. It's already starting to show a lot..."

"It doesn't show too much..." Michael lied to her as he blushed more than he should.

"Come on, Michael. It has only been a day since you bred me and I already have a pronounced belly. What have you done to me?" she turned to him and asked him.

"Um..." he scratched the back of his head, feeling embarrassed and even a bit nervous, "I don't really know..." he added, having absolutely no idea how this pregnancy was progressing so fast.

"You bred me so hard..." she erotically whispered into his ear, therefore, turning him on in public in the middle of the street.

"Umn... Well..." he shrugged his shoulders, "maybe we should tell everyone about the werewolf attack and all these shadows... It's getting out of hand..." Michael changed the subject to something that needed to be dealt with immediately.

*Bang!*

"No! We can't tell anyone!" Maleva suddenly turned against him and violently pushed him against a brick wall after swiftly lifting him off the ground. She wouldn't have been able to do something like that with everyone watching, so she smoothly pulled him into a back alley right before lifting him and pushing him against the wall.

"Huh! Mal? What's wrong with you?"

"In case you didn't notice yet, we're wolves. We are just as much werewolves as the one who wants us dead. Besides, we don't know its identity yet and it could be anyone in town, so we have to be as careful as possible. Do you understand me?" she threatened her childhood friend as she held him up against that wall.

"But we still have to warn people about the danger..."

The two clearly didn't see eye-to-eye on this matter.

"It's *not* safe to do so!" she pushed him even harder against the brick wall and nearly choked him to death with the rough way she held him there. However, there was one positive note in all of this: Her big chest was so close to his that her breasts were accidentally being squished in his chest and even in his face a bit. Turned out that the choking was also caused by her pillow-tits!

"I... Am... Not... Going... To... Let... You... Do... This... I'll... Warn... Everyone... About... The... Menace..." he kept confronting her.

Silence.

"Ahaha..."

Maleva soon broke the silence with an adorable giggle.

"What's wrong with you?" the young boy questioned her.

"You know what? You're pretty cute when you stand up for what you believe in. So cute, in fact, that I feel like... Kissing you right now..." she did. Maleva leaned forward while continuing to kiss him.

*Smack!*

A wet kiss right on the lips.

Then, she introduced her pink tongue inside of his mouth and their kiss became that much more sexual. Their tongues rolled with one another inside of his mouth.

The deal was sealed at this point. Lust was so aroused that she wasn't going to let this go now. She wanted him. She was craving him. This was going to happen. Right here in the back alley in public, no one could see them.

Maleva finally placed the young boy back down on his feet.

The childhood friend undressed herself. Took off her orange thong. Pulled her giant tits out of her red and green tunic. She then raised her left leg as high as possible in the air and had her foot pushing against the brick wall, so her entire thigh was over him.

Her wet pussy was revealed to him.

She wasted no time to pull his pants and boxers down and his hard cock bobbed right outside.

Unable to resist him, she used his erect dick and had her slippery wet pussy lips collide with his cockhead!

*Slip!*

His cock sloppily made it inside of her lovely pussy and they began fucking right there in the back alley!

Anyone could see them and find out about what they were doing if they were to get close enough to them.

"Ahn! Ahn! Yes! Michael! Your cock feels better every day!" she moaned as they just started to have sex in public.

This was going to be a quick one.

A quickie in the back alley.

Her big tits bounced up and down as she sucked his dick with her pussy. Pulling outward and inward in a loop in the hope of satisfying herself using his dick. The satisfaction was almost instant. She felt so satisfied that she could already come any second now... Michael's cock felt amazing to her.

"It's a good thing Lycanna is not with us and that she was sleeping when we headed out... Ahn..." Maleva mentioned right before going back to moaning some more.

"I was serious before, Mal. I'm going to tell people about the danger surrounding Cherrywood," he reminded her that this was a serious path that he was going to take.

"I know you are! Ahn! I'm coming! You're going to make me come, Michael!"

The time had come!

Maleva's pussy pulsated until she ultimately came!

Her orgasm was so massively important and pleasurable to her, that she couldn't afford to pull any of her moaning back.

"Wwwwee! Ahn! Weemnee! Ahn! Mmn!" she moaned as loud as she wished to, even though they were out in public.

Lactation!

Fresh milk was squirted out of her thick nipples at the same time she came!

"I'm cumming as well!" Michael lashed out.

Her pussy made him come so hard as well!

The young boy filled her up again!

Breeding her again!

# Chapter 20: The Bad Wolf Is Back

That night was a rainy one.

The shadow werewolf covered in beautiful dead Autumn leaves knocked at the door of Cherrywood.

Through the darkness of the night, it infiltrated itself in this innocent, small, and pure community.

*Among us.*

It took one random member of the community who just happened to be walking in one of the streets of the village: A woman. A mother. A wife. A loved one.

The hunt was short but sweet. The beast tore it apart with ease and disposed of its body. The blood was being washed away by the rain. The woman never had any time to scream. It was over before he knew what happened.

It wasn't even a full night tonight.

It was still a crescent moon, but the moon could barely be seen in the dark sky because of these black clouds and all this rain everywhere.

***

At the foster home in Cherrywood, Michael once again snuck Maleva, the huntress inside his room, although he wasn't supposed to bring anyone. Lycanna thankfully once again gave them the room as she squatted in the living room where she could get comfy.

"I love being pregnant with you, Michael," she let him know again.

"How does it feel?"

"Fantastic! It feels so great to be having puppies growing inside of me! *Your* puppies," she corrected herself.

"I think that I'm more human than beast, so how do you know you're going to have puppies? How does it work with werewolves, really?" She kept talking about puppies over and over again to the point that he no longer knew if she was exaggerating or not.

"I really don't want to repeat myself, but I'm a pure-blood werewolf and even though you're half-blood, you're still a werewolf, Michael. So, they're definitely going to be puppies," she confidently explained to him as she shared his tiny single bed with him.

"Speaking of being a wolf..." Maleva turned to the window. Saw the crescent moon in the dark sky, even though it was so hard to see because of all these clouds and rain, which constantly hit the window glass at quite a calming pace. The same kind of pace that she needed in order to transform back into the wolf girl that she was!

By the time Maleva turned back to the young man, she had already turned into a werewolf. The wolf ears, irises, fangs, claws, as well as the wolf tail, everything was there.

She was back as a werewolf.

Then, she leaned forward and kissed her man right on the lips. She soon inserted her long and sensual wolf tongue inside of his mouth. During the French kiss, Michael also transformed into the beast because of the effect that the moon also had on him.

Wolf ears, fangs, claws, and a tail. A wolf boy.

The wolf boy and girl were united in these bestial forms again. The horny fun could finally begin. Maleva had already stripped out of her clothes long before she ever turned that night. The same was not the case for her boy, though.

"These go off!" she aggressively announced to him at the same time as she violently pulled on his clothes and ripped them apart with her sharp claws.

Two seconds later, Michael was entirely naked with his clothes in shreds falling down in slow-motion everywhere around and on the bed.

Then, it was when she finally saw his big and hard cock again that she truly knew what she wanted to do to him tonight. In a flash—Maleva moved her entire thick and heavy body around and directly showed her big ass and pussy to him! Right to his face! Meanwhile, she found herself face-to-face with his huge boner. She executed her plan to perfection and had her massively large tits sitting on both sides of his member.

His rod was right between her wolf tits!

"How about this?" she asked him as she used her breasts as ultra-soft pillows for his cock and massaged it with them. A titty-fuck? This was exactly what it was, but she was in full control of what was happening. Her boobs were so large and thick that she didn't even need to move them around with her hands in order to massage his cock. She only needed to move her chest and that was it.

"A titty massage just for you, my beautiful wolf boy! Ahn!"

"Um... Maleva..." Michael felt like he was in Heaven right now.

"I want to pleasure you as much as possible, Michael. Ahn! It's necessary for me to thank you for everything you've done for me, starting by breeding me. Mhn! You're making me so happy. Mmng!" she couldn't stop moaning as she spoke to him.

However, this wasn't all. Maleva had something else up her sleeves. She leaned forward during the breast massage and opened her mouth. With her eyes shut, she stuck her long tongue out of her mouth and began licking the tip of his cockhead! Then, she went deeper with it, completely sucking on his glans as she lay down on top of him.

Meanwhile, the boy couldn't resist her wet pussy, which had been offered on a silver platter right in front of him (better be careful with mentioning the word 'silver', though). Michael soon had his tongue swinging around from the left to the right as he tasted her wonderful vagina! He even went pretty deep inside of her pussy with this tongue, making it an interesting penetration that Maleva was definitely going to remember for a long, long time afterward.

*He's licking my pussy! He's inside of my pussy with his tongue! I'm coming! I'm coming!* Maleva couldn't even speak because she had his dick in her mouth.

However, this didn't prevent her from coming as hard as she did at that moment as her man ate her!

"Mal! I'm cumming! I'm cumming!"

Then, it was the wolf boy's turn!

Even though he had enough time to warn her, he still strongly ejaculated inside of her mouth. Unloading everything inside and having her swallow it all up! Eating his semen!

*I love you, Michael...* she admitted to herself. Something that she wasn't able to say out loud to him.

\*\*\*

The big, bad wolf's hunt wasn't over yet.

The shadow werewolf was still present in Cherrywood.

It lurked right outside the foster home.

Perfectly knowing who was inside.

\*\*\*

Meanwhile, Lycanna, the wolf spirit, was wide awake in the living room of the foster home.

Standing.

Looking outside.

Understanding the enemy was right there at the door.

"This is soon about to get a lot worse..." Lycanna murmured to herself.

Camille Juteau

She knew what was coming.

# Chapter 21: The Little Red Riding Hood

The next hunt was about to begin!

It was about time too!

First and foremost: Maleva had been summoned to the town's hall relatively early in the morning. Probably much earlier than needed, but that was beside the point.

Here, at town hall, she met the head of the town of Cherrywood.

Who was she?

While she assumed the role of mayor for the small town, she was more recognized as the head huntress of Cherrywood. And to be honest, she was the only huntress in town with Maleva. Then, Michael would have been considered the third hunter, but this was about it for the people of Cherrywood who could actually hunt.

"Did it really have to be this early?" Maleva asked the head of Cherrywood, scratching her eyes because she was so tired.

Michael was here as well. He stood behind Maleva. Just as exhausted as she was. The boy's hair was all messed up and spiking in the air. This was not great, but he hadn't taken any time to look at himself in the mirror first before heading out. Thankfully, his right eye was still covered by his long hair, which made him cute and handsome. Especially to most girls and women he met, including Maleva, Lycanna, and other ladies he encountered every day in town. It was fair to say that most girls found him adorable, yet, he wished to be taken a bit more seriously. He should have been taken more seriously because of his cursed and bestial nature, but no one knew that he was a wolf, so that didn't help him to be taken seriously at all.

"Um... I see that you brought your boyfriend with you..." The chief huntress of Cherrywood soon noticed the young man behind her.

The older woman was in her early forties.

She had bright green eyes. Long, orange-brown hair with large bangs.

She was a perfect MILF in all the ways imaginable.

Breasts were even larger than Maleva's. Michael had no idea that was even possible in the first place. A thick buttery ass. Wide hips and thick thighs.

*What? Does she think I'm her boyfriend?*

"He's not my boyfriend! This is not what you think!" Maleva was in full panic mode now.

"Then, why do you follow him everywhere you go and vice-versa?" the chief huntress pointed out to her.

"Um... This is not exactly it..." Michael desperately attempted to calm things down, but this was all in vain.

"Well, I think the two of you make for a formidable couple!" the chief huntress gave her opinion on the matter as she smiled. She was so happy for the two of them

"Mom! I swear to God! Don't talk about stuff you don't understand!" Maleva nearly burst into a million pieces she was blushing so much. It was at that moment that she revealed an important piece of information Michael had no idea about...

*Mom? This is her mother?* Michael realized it a bit too late. Now that he looked at her with different eyes, he could now finally see that this woman looked a lot like Maleva.

"She's your mom?" Michael asked Maleva, marvelously shocked.

"Yeah. So, what?" Maleva turned to the young man.

"Alright, alright, I won't keep talking about your couple, Mal. I understand this is your social life and not mine. So, let's get back to the important topic at hand—the reason why I woke the both of you so early this morning!"

"Yes, mother. Please tell us what this important mission is going to be about and what we'll need to accomplish on this hunt..." Maleva was dying to know.

"A mission?" Michael asked.

*I thought it was going to be a normal hunt. But now it's a mission? What does that even mean?* The young man asked himself.

...

It was pure silence for a long time in the room as they waited for her instructions...

What was this important mission all about...?

...

"So... Would you mind taking this cake and this bottle of wine to your grandma out of town for me, dear?" Maleva's mother politely and sweetly asked her.

...

Another silence followed...

Maleva's jaw dropped!

Michae's did too...

*This is her important mission?* The boy asked himself.

"Mom... Did you wake us up this early for something like that? It's not even four in the morning yet. And I thought this was going to be an important mission. What happened to the important mission?" Maleva questioned her own mother as she questioned her.

"This is your important mission..." she repeated to her.

"This isn't so bad... We should be back soon, right...?" Michael still found some positive in having to do this mundane task for her mother.

"I'm sure you'll do great! Thank you so much, guys!"

"Hold up! Wait a minute there, Mom! I thought that you were going to ask us to do something related to the Moonlit Sins or something like that! I thought you had located one of the sins!" Maleva fully revealed what she had originally expected of her. Her hopes and dreams!

*Wait... What? Mal just spoke out loud about the sins! So, that must mean that her mom knows about them, too? Wait a minute! This just crossed my mind! Mal is a pure-blood werewolf, so that also means that... Her mom is also a werewolf! Another pure-blood wolf!* Michael finally realized the gravity of the situation!

"Not yet, dear. I'll let you know when I locate another sin like you," her mother casually told her, smiling the entire time she spoke to her.

"It better be soon! I've waited years for this! I just desperately want to find another sin like me!" Maleva shouted out loud in the room. Her voice echoing and bouncing back off the walls.

"In time. It'll be soon. I'm sure of it. There. Take this," her mother handed her a cute red basket.

Maleva was just about to reluctantly accept it and take it when—

—*I should be the one to hold it for her!* Michael thought at the last second.

He swiftly took the basket off of the mother's hands before Maleva ever could.

"Um?" Maleva had no idea why he did this.

"I should be the one holding it for you, Mal," Michael insisted.

"Oh! Such a gallant young man! I love it!" the chief huntress blushed. She began liking it even more already.

"Whatever. We should go now. See you later, mom!" Maleva spun around and left with her childhood friend.

"Oh! Mal! I almost forgot this..."

They stopped.

Turned around.

Her mother handed something else to her: Clothes. They were a red hood and a red cape.

"It's going to be cold in the woods today, you should take this..."

"Thanks, mom..."

Maleva reluctantly accepted the hood and the cape. Taking them.

\*\*\*

The chief huntress was right.

It was pretty cold once they stepped back outside.

It was freezing, in fact.

It was snowy, too.

When Maleva stepped outside with Michael, she now had the red hood and cape on.

She was adorable and sexy in this outfit. Especially with the hood up.

"Mal..."

"What?" she asked him.

"You look so beautiful in that outfit..."

She blushed. A lot.

"Let's go..." she looked away and led the way...

# Chapter 22: Going Into The Woods

"So, your mom knows about the Moonlit Sins?"

"Of course, she knows! She's one of the only few people who do. Why did you think that I didn't want you to tell regular people in Cherrywood the other day? Not everyone could know about this. Not everyone can know about me and you being wolves. You know?" Michael and Maleva walked side-by-side on a beaten path in the woods. The same woods they were recently attacked in by the third werewolf.

"Is your mom a sin?" Michael asked her the question he had been dying to ask her even since they left town.

"No. She's not."

"But then, she's still a werewolf, right? You said it yourself before. You're a pure-blood. So, that means that everyone that has your blood is also a werewolf..." The young boy presented his theory to her.

"You're pretty smart, Michael. I like that," she smiled at him.

"I'm not smart. I'm only attentive. That's all," he pointed out to her.

"Waf!" they both suddenly heard a dog or a wolf playfully barking behind them.

They turned around to discover that the animal who just barked at them was no other than Lycanna! She ran on all fours, something she didn't always do, and quickly came their way. More specially, she came to Michael and adorably rubbed herself all over his right leg. It came across as if it had been a little while since she had seen him.

She wagged her tail as she finally reunited with him.

Her tongue sticking out of her mouth and flailing around.

"Lycanna?"

"Guess she missed you..." Maleva mentioned, shrugging.

"Missed you!" Lycanan could be heard as she continued wagging her tail.

Michael bent over to pet her head and she loved it.

"Never had a dog before—guess this must be how it feels to have one..." he always wished he had one when he was a bit younger.

"You're definitely making up for all that time you spent without one. You know? While being one yourself now and everything," This made Maleva laugh a bit She chuckled as she placed one hand in front of her mouth. Almost relishing in the fact that her childhood friend was now a wolf just like her. Since she had always been one, it was a great, personal pleasure to have Michael join her. Be a wolf with her. They were also in the same pack now. They were together. United. Linked. Even if they were not boyfriend and girlfriend yet, they were still linked as they were in the same wolf pack.

Lycanna continued rubbing her head all over his foot as a new presence was soon detected in the area...

*Sniff!*

Michael was the first one who was able to smell that a stranger was nearby...

"Someone's here!"

*Sniff! Sniff!*

"Yes. I can smell it, as well," Maleva agreed.

*Sniff...*

Lycanna also smelled in the hope of having a better idea as to what they were dealing with... Unfortunately for her, whatever was hiding in the woods sprung out on them a bit too fast and surprised the wolf spirit!

"Wuf-wof!" Lycanna barked at whatever was about to come out of the bushes. Trying to intimidate the intruder. Yet, this, unfortunately, didn't work out too much as a shadow quickly lept above the grasses and harshly struck Lycanna!

*Bang!*

"Ugh!" the little wolf made a sad puppy noise when she was sadly hit.

Violently hitting her head and launching her in the air! Lycanna's body hit another tree hard!

"Lycanna!" Michael shouted.

"No!" Maleva felt so bad she allowed this to happen in the first place.

The shadowy presence did not remain a shadow for too long. It revealed itself to be a vile creature. The beast was a strange demon wolf. A wolf that walked on four legs, but was much larger than a regular one, and possessed no eyes. Yet, it could still see pretty well.

"What is that thing?" Michael asked.

"No idea."

Then, the demonic wolf soon rushed toward Lycanna again. Much like it was the case recently with the other shadows when they came back to town after spending some time at the farm.

Michael and Maleva had to act now, otherwise, Lycanna was doomed.

Maleva moved first: She ran toward the demonic wolf and threw a hunting knife at it. She did not miss and managed to hit it right on the side of his neck. However, it did very little to slow it down during its run to attack the wolf spirit again.

It was Michael's chance to do something.

He charged at the demon wolf and placed himself right between it and Lycanna.

The demonic wolf roared in dominance as it saw that Michael was truly trying to stop it, risking his life for her. Now, that the young boy had its attention, this was the most perfect opportunity for the huntress to get in its back. She did so and prepared another hunting knife.

She ran as fast as she could to stop the demonic wolf from attacking Michael, but the enemy was too fast for her.

"Come to me!" Meanwhile, Michael encouraged the demonic wolf to attack him. This was not exactly what Maleva wanted him to do since it was so dangerous and he could get killed, but at least, this gave her a chance to surprise the creature. Still, she had to catch it first...

"Kaaaaarr!" the demonic wolf roared one more time.

It was too late.

It was about to assault Michael. Maleva was still too far.

*Chomp!*

The demon wolf had finally made its move.

With its mouth wide open, it took a chunk out of Michael!

But did it?

Blood was drawn.

"Michael!"

Maleva thought Michael had been bitten for sure, but when she looked up, she realized that this was not exactly the case...

Michael sacrificed himself by having his hands injured, but he managed to stop the beast by keeping its mouth open. His right hand had the upper half of its mouth open, while his left hand did the same for the lower half.

His hands were cut.

Blood dripped down his fingers...

The courageous young man continued holding the demon's mouth open...

"Michael..."

"So, what are you waiting for, Mal? Are you going to come help me or what?" Michael grunted, barely able to fight the beast off anymore since it was so strong...

"Y-yes! I'm on it!"

The beautiful huntress then lept in the air and landed right on the back of the four-legged demon.

She pulled her hunting knife out and slit the demon's throat!

Ending its reign of terror.

However, this was only another member of the shadow werewolf's pack.

The pack was still out there.

Still after them...

# Chapter 23: Bonfire Time

At night, Michael and Maleva lit up a bonfire while watching over Lycanna, who was still resting following the attack.

"Is she going to be alright?" Michael asked, worried about how badly Lycanna was hit.

"She'll be fine. I've seen worse. Nothing is broken. She should be able to walk when she wakes up in the morning," she explained to him.

"If she can't, I'll carry her myself. I feel responsible for what happened to her somehow," Michael felt responsible for everything that kept happening related to the dark creatures they encountered in these woods.

"It's not your fault. This thing came out of nowhere as soon as we left town and went straight for Lycanna... This was also the case not too long ago when we came back from the farm. I really don't know what it is. They seemed to be after her more than they were us. I really wish I knew," the huntress replied to him as she lay down right next to the warm and soothing bonfire. Her curves were perfectly highlighted by the flames. Her back and her big ass touched the ground, but not most of her legs except for her feet. Her forearms resting on her knees. She was still wearing all of her clothes at that time, but she laid so close to the bonfire that this was definitely something that was bound to change sooner or later...

"I swear to find out why they are after her. I promise to bring this werewolf and his pack down!" Michael was determined to make this happen.

Maleva was too, but there was something else she was slightly more interested in doing right about now...

Not noticing her doing so at first, the young woman with the red and green hair started to strip right next to the hot flames. She began by removing her tunic and then slowly pulled on her fishnet top until it was completely down...

*Boing! Boing!*

Her big tits jiggled freely as she got rid of the fishnet top. Then, the only thing that was still covering her tits, masking her nipples to be accurate, was her wolf paw-shaped nipple covers. They were definitely next on the list...

"Um... What are you doing, Mal?" Michael finally noticed what she was in the middle of executing.

"It's just that I'm so hot because of our bonfire. I think we might have overdone it. Wouldn't you say so?" she replied to him with the most seductive, soft, and erotic voice she could pull off. She was telling the truth though, she was sweating so much that sweat was dripping right between her big boobs. She also had to keep fanning herself with her right hand in order to stay somewhat stable and not burn right out.

"Well, you're right next to the fire, Mal," the young boy pointed out to her.

*Zzzzzz...*

"Listen. Lycanna's snoring. I'm feeling like I am in heat again. Do you mind if we have sex before going to bed?" Maleva finally asked him the question that she had on her lips for the past half hour or so.

*What? She wants to have sex again? Wow! I am so lucky to be spending so much time with her! She wants to have sex all the time! I definitely do not mind, at all!* Deeply aroused, Michael instantly became erect as soon as he heard what she just asked him.

Michael was so excited that he was momentarily lost in his train of thought as reflected on how awesome Maleva was. He stayed silent until...

"So... What do you say... Do you mind...?"

"Um... Yeah, you know? If you really want to, I mean..." Michael shrugged. Pretending like this was not such a big deal to him.

"Thank you, Michael... But I want to try something different today..."

"Um... What is it...?" he asked with lots of curiosity.

*Plop!*

Maleva responded by pulling on her right nipple cover and removing it from her boob, revealing her exposed nipple to him. Exciting him that much more

"My nipples are really hard tonight... The interior of them is gaping as well. Look. It's almost as if they are opening up. The opening of my nipples is so wide that your cock would almost fit inside, wouldn't you say?" Maleva blushed as she began explaining what she wished the young boy to do to her.

*She has to be kidding me... Mal is honestly asking me to do something this strange and perverted to her?*

"So, you want me to make love with your nipple?" he asked her

"Yes... Please..." she begged him

In the short amount of time that it took him to walk up to her, he had already become hard enough to perform that task that she so politely asked of him. Two seconds later, Maleva pulled his pants down and his delicious cock throbbed out in the open!

Aroused, Maleva stroked his dick for a short amount before bringing her tit as close as possible to the tip of his head.

She delicately pulled on his member and had his glans rubbing all over the exterior of her nipple. A pure flesh connection. The boy was already producing and secreting a colossal amount of pre-cum out of his cock, so he covered her boob in it in no time.

Maleva attempted to push his head inside of her nipple several times, but the actual task ended up being a lot harder than she thought it was going to be...

"Please work... Please work..." She tried time and time again and it wouldn't work. It wouldn't fit inside until...

"Let me do it," until Michael did it himself.

He pushed his dick against the tip of her nipple until it finally entered inside!

*Sleek!*

Michael was finally inside of her boob! He penetrated her nipple with sloppiness and pure perversion.

"Ahn! Yes! That's exactly what I've been fantasizing about for a long time! Mhn!" She bit her lower lip, inflicting a bit of pain on herself she was so aroused.

She almost came across as if she was going to come right away after he first penetrated her nipple with his cock.

Her thick and erect nipple acted like a suction tube for his member.

Getting used to being inside of her nipple, he moved his dick back and forth. Doing so a bit faster with every second that passed.

"I meant to try nipple penetration for the longest time! Oh! Yes! I'm coming! I'm coming so hard!" she shouted next to the bonfire.

She couldn't help it.

Maleva had already come.

Just as aroused as she was, Michael also came!

The young boy ejaculated inside of her nipple! Not expecting this to feel as good as it did.

*Sploosh!*

"I'm coming inside of your nipple, Mal!"

His semen quickly overflowed out of her nipple!

It was a miracle that Lycanna didn't wake up at all as the two of them did this perverted thing in the wilderness.

# Chapter 24: Grandma's House

The next day, they reached Grandma's house in the middle of the woods.

*Knock! Knock! Knock!*

They heard footsteps on the other side. It was faint, but they heard it. The doorknob was turned and the door was finally opened...

Grandma was coming...

As Michael fully expected to discover an old woman with plenty of ridges and looking much older than Maleva's mom, he was shocked to be met with a lady who didn't look old at all. She didn't look much older than Maleva's mother, actually.

Her grandma didn't look like a grandma, at all. In order to be a grandma, she obviously had to be a bit older than her daughter, but she still came across as if she was in her early forties or late thirties.

Grandma was one thick woman!

She was a massively big, beautiful woman with only thick forms to her, as well as an actual chubby stomach, which made her somehow even more gorgeous and seductive. Michael had no idea, but this was indeed the feeling that he had while seeing her for the first time. Perhaps this was the natural and organic and perfect MILF aura that she oozed off with her presence.

If Maleva's mother had bigger breasts than her, grandma possessed breasts even larger! Her wide hips, ass, and thick thighs were also things to not take lightly.

The front door of her house was swung wide open!

And this was how *Aurora* was introduced to Michael!

She looked at the young boy with her beautiful orange eyes. However, one of the things that attracted him the most was her snow-white hair, which came down to her shoulders, which was simply remarkably enticing with her gorgeous dark skin tone.

"Welcome home!" The woman with the white hair welcomed them with open arms, "Maleva! I missed you so much!" She then turned her head to Michael, "It's a pleasure to meet you, young man I've heard so many great things about you," she added as she soon set eyes on him for the first time.

"You did...?" Michael virtually had no idea what to say, at all.

"Hello, grandma," Maleva was glad to be here. It had been a while since she visited her grandma.

"Maleva! You've grown so much since the last time I saw you!"

"I did?" Maleva wasn't too sure.

She then turned to the young boy again.

"The name is Redheart, right? Michael Redheart?" she asked him to be sure she got it right.

"That's it, ma'am..." he grew pretty shy in her presence.

"Allow me to introduce myself—my name is Aurora."

*Aurora? I never met anyone with a name like that before... It's pretty unique and suits her well... Damn! Is she really a granny or are they pranking me? She's so hot! Her tits are the biggest ones I have ever seen in my entire life... How did they get as large as they are? It's incredible...* right off the bat, Michael had so many thoughts about this gorgeous woman he just met.

"It's... It's an honor to meet you Aurora, I mean, ma'am..." he corrected himself at the last second, not meaning to miss her in any respect.

"No, Aurora is fine. No, ma'am," she clarified with him.

"Understood, ma'am... I mean... Aurora..."

Aurora chuckled, placing one hand in front of her lips as she did. Enjoying herself already while the young man was sweating his ass off over there, desperately attempting to make a good impression.

Michael couldn't take his eyes off of the motherly outfit that Aurora wore: A bright green dress with a violet apron attached around her waists. Green toeless high-heels.

"Welcome on in! We'll have some of that cake you came to bring in the first place!" Aurora welcomed them inside of her home in the middle of the woods.

\*\*\*

"I see that your mom handed you the red hood," Aurora mentioned to her granddaughter as the three of them gathered around a vintage wooden circular table in her cozy dining room, which also doubled as the living room since her cabin was so tiny. So tiny that it added a lot of charm to the place by having everyone so close to one another. This small cabin was filled with love and it was oozing from it. Everyone was gathered around to have some pie. It was still too early for wine, but...

"She did," Maleva confirmed.

"What's so special about the red hood, anyway?" Michael asked, becoming a bit more curious since it was true that Maleva hadn't stopped wearing it ever since they set foot out of Cherrywood after her mother gave it to her along with the bottle of wine and the cake.

...

No one said anything about it. None of them seemed to want to reply to him for some reason.

"So, Michael, I hear that my granddaughter is truly fond of you, is that true?" this was more than enough to make him blush and nearly have blood gush out of his nose!

"I guess..." Michael had no idea what to say.

"Is this the best thing to say, Aurora?" Maleva asked her.

*She referred to her grandma as Aurora. I'm now beginning to wonder if 'grandma' isn't just some title or something like that... Perhaps she's not even her real Grandma... Not that it really matters anyway...* the young man thought to himself.

"Sure is because I am just as fond of him as you are," Aurora seductively gazed at Michael as she turned to him.

*What the hell did she just say? My heart is melting! What is going on? I'm beginning to feel my cock rising beneath the table! What am I going to do? What's happening on this strange mission?*

"Aurora! This is out of line!" Maleva immediately reacted. Feeling more jealous than ever it seemed.

"It's not. I'm just really excited about this young boy..." she claimed.

*That young boy was me... I'm dying over here on the other side of the table...*

"There, Aurora. We brought you your cake and your bottle of wine. Our mission is done here," Maleva announced as she stood up, slightly furious.

*Meanwhile, as all of this is going on and I have no idea what to do, really, I feel a strange presence right outside the cabin... There is something lurking around... It smells just like.... It smells just like the mysterious werewolf who is after me and Maleva. Lycanna is outside. This means that she's in danger. I have to do something!*

# Chapter 25: Aurora

At night, Michael could still feel the presence of the shadow werewolf outside the cabin.

The big, bad, wolf was still roaming around in the woods. Awaiting the perfect opportunity to strike. This had for effect to prevent the young boy from falling asleep and getting the rest he so deserved. This also had the effect of making him a lot more nervous. Michael was not doing well at all. He was left scratching the skin of his arms a lot. Scratching and pulling on his hair sometimes. Biting his lip. Doing this he shouldn't really do to himself because he was just that nervous because of that threat outside that he didn't know if he should tell the others about just yet...

However, all of these fears and nervousness vanished as soon as...

*Creeeeaaak...*

...!

The door of his bedroom slowly opened...

Everyone was sleeping in a different room tonight. Three separate rooms for three different people.

*Someone's coming inside the room... Maleva?*

Michael fully opened his eyes and realized that it was not Maleva, but Aurora, instead, who came inside his room in the middle of the night.

Aurora slowly walked up to his bed and sat on the edge of it. Joining him in bed.

*Aurora? What is she doing in my room?*

"Michael."

...

"I know you're not asleep, Michael," she added after pausing for two seconds.

*Does she know I'm not asleep? Better say something to her, now. Anything...*

"Ma'am...? Not able to fall asleep, huh?" the young man finally addressed her, opening his eyes again and witnessing the beauty of the older and more mature woman sitting in bed with him, seductively staring at him.

He soon discovered that she was now only wearing a thin silver nightgown, which was so see-through that it allowed him to pretty much see everything she was presenting to him, including her big tits, her areolae, her nipples, and even a bit of her thick stomach.

However, he couldn't see her pussy, since she had her legs seductively folded together.

*HER NIGHTGOWN! SHE'S NEARLY NAKED!*

"I'd like to kiss you, Michael," Aurora politely asked him.

*Kiss me?*

"Why would you want to do that?"

"Kiss you goodnight? Well, just so you can sleep better my dear..."

...

"Then... I guess, it's okay..."

Sliding up to him, Aurora quickly went ahead and kissed the young boy right on the lips. Probably one of the most sensual kisses of his entire life. Her tongue slipped into his mouth, not by accident, of course, and it then twirled all around his. A French kiss that he was not going to forget anytime soon.

Her ample chest was also firmly pressed against his. Her tits squished against his body.

It was at that moment that she felt something pretty pronounced and hard between his legs as she moved that much closer to him.

"Um?"

She looked down... And it was his big and hard dick. The boy was erect. She had done this to him.

"I'm sorry..." Michael had pretty much no idea how to react to an older and more mature woman doing this sort of thing with him. Caring for him like a mother, but even going a bit deeper with it. Being extra.

Aurora pulled his hard cock out of his pants and kept her hand all around his shaft as she held it.

She jerked the young boy off and she was comfortable doing so, even though this came out of absolutely nowhere from Michael's point of view. However, this didn't mean that he didn't like it. Far from it

"Ma'am? What are you doing?"

"Aurora's fine. Please call me Aurora. You make me feel so old," she chuckled, messing with him, having a blast with him.

"Aurora. Does Maleva know you're here?" He was suspicious that she came here to his room without her knowledge and this smelled fishy to him. Why was she here to begin with? What was going on?

But instead of answering him, she stroked his throbbing dick a few more times and this soon caused it to erupt. Pre-cum overflowed from the top of his cock.

The apparition of pre-cum then accidentally led to...

The young man partially shifted back into a beast! The wolf boy had been brought back! Wolf ears and a tail suddenly came out of his body. He was also armed with dangerous fangs and deadly claws, even though he didn't need them right now. Then, sharp irises in his eyes.

He was transforming into a wolf. Not exactly in his complete werewolf form yet, but his wolf-boy appearance had been fully installed on him as the mature lady continued stroking his dick. Pre-cum came out of the top of his cock. More than ever.

She noticed his transformation as soon as it took over him.

*No! She's going to know...*

"Look at that. I know for a fact that you were a wolf the second you showed up at my cabin," Aurora admired the wolf boy with pleasant and attentive eyes.

She was surely lusting for him.

A few more strokes of his cock and...

There he came!

Michael shot his load as a wolf boy. Cumming all over her hand and his own rod.

*I came so much...*

"Good work, my lovely. Your semen is so warm," she congratulated him like a sweet mother would do.

*She's happy I came?*

"Wish we could do more right now, but I really need to take a walk outside. It's too hot here. Give me two minutes, would you?"

"No, that's probably a bad idea. You shouldn't go outside. I felt something earlier..."

"Don't worry. I know these woods like the back of my hand. Besides, I'm *not* twelve. I'll be just fine, you know?" she told him.

"No, please, don't go outside..." he begged her, but it was too late.

Aurora gently smiled at him before standing up and soon leaving, closing the door behind her, and excitingly licking the sperm off of her fingers.

She was gone.

Gone outside in the darkness

***

When she came back, it was bright and early in the morning.

Aurora was found by Michael and Maleva, lying in her own bed. Eyes wide opened. Looking more or less normal in appearance, but, unfortunately, no longer having a soul.

"What happened to her?" Maleva asked the young man.

"She went outside in the middle of the night..." Michael replied to her.

They had to help her.

They had to do something for her.

# Chapter 26: Saving Her Soul

"You've got to do something to help her!" Maleva urged him to help her.

"I get that, but what do you want me to do, exactly?"

"You're going to have to restore her soul," she explained to him.

"Restore her soul? But how? Why am I the only one who can do it...?"

"Because we need a male to do this sort of thing..." she admitted to him.

*A male is needed to do this sort of thing? I'm not even sure where she's going with that... How can I restore her soul, really?*

*...*

*Then, it came to me... Everything was making a lot of sense, now...*

Aurora lay in a seductive position in her bed. Her buxom attributes were lying on their sides and her ass was nearly sticking out of the mattress. Her blanket was not even covering her properly.

"Come on, look at her, Michael. She's not herself. Her soul was damaged. The rogue werewolf probably did this last night. We have to save her, but only a male can do so. I see no other option, Michael. You're going to have to have sex with her," Maleva announced to him.

*I need to have sex with her to save her!*

"Are you sure?" Michael asked her.

"Yes... Please do it..." she begged him.

"Very well then..." the boy stepped forward. Finally approaching the bed.

"Maleva's right... You have to do it..." Aurora somehow managed to speak for the first time since she had been placed in this catatonic state. Like this, she wasn't able to close her eyes. She wasn't able to move much, but the real Aurora was still somehow in there. She figured a way to move just enough, so she could undo her blouse and open it up: Revealing her wondrous big tits to the young boy, which were even larger than what Maleva had.

"Aurora?" the young man's eyes grew wide. Excitement. Pure arousal came over him.

"Um..." Even Maleva, the girl, who was supposed to be her granddaughter received a strong reaction to seeing her naked... Her big and free tits jiggled in all directions as they were exposed for Michael.

Upon reaching her bed, the boy climbed on it to rescue her. Moved as close as he could to her without crawling over her too much in fear of hurting her, even though he shouldn't fear such a thing, she was a much larger and thicker woman than Maleva was. Finally, with her, she requested a kiss, wetting her own lips and appetite for him. He knew what he had to do next... They kissed.

This kiss felt much different from the ones he had with Maleva. Her lips were thick and just as soft as it was the case for her supposed grandmother. One kiss alone was more than enough for him to become hard. Heavily erect. She felt his member against her stomach since it was throbbing so much. She couldn't say anything about it because she was still cursed and she couldn't behave as normal, unfortunately. It was up to Michael to fix this since he was the only male around.

"Do it, Michael... Please do it... Make love to her..." Maleva begged him.

"Yes... Please make love to me..." While she wasn't able to do a lot right now, Aurora was still about to ask for this favor. Furthermore, she was also able to move a bit, so she lay down on her back a bit better and spread her long legs for him. Her nightgown was lifted!

*The light shone on him!*

There it was: Her beautiful pink pussy right there in his face as she would pass her thick thighs behind her head as she offered herself to him. The young man then moved closer to her. His cock now throbbing right between her legs.

He knew what he had to do and if Aurora's life depended on it, he had to do everything to restore the balance of her soul. Heck! Michael would still do it if her life wasn't on the line and she only asked him to make love to her, anyway!

Here it goes...

The young man leaned forward and rubbed the tip of his cock all across Aurora's pussy lips. Preparing for an eventual penetration. He couldn't wait to do so, but one of the things that he was looking forward to the most was definitely doing some lewd and nasty stuff to her big tits. He still couldn't wrap his mind around it: Soft breasts larger than what Maleva already had.

This still didn't feel like something that could be true, so in order to make sure that this wasn't a dream or anything like that, Michael shoved his face right between her milf titis and rubbed it all over them before beginning to kiss them with a fiery passion.

*They smell and taste so wonderful!*

However, the young man still had to make love to her pussy in the hope of saving her soul, but he still wasn't quite inside. So, Aurora then went ahead and did the only reasonable thing: She swiftly got a hold of his big, throbbing cock and plunged right into the mature woman's vagina. Finally making the final connection between the two. She helped out however she could. Building that bridge between the two of them.

It was time to break the curse!

"Ahn... This is exactly what I need... This is already helping..." Aurora moaned as the boy fucked her with all he had and sucked on her delicious nipples at the same time. Much like many women with huge breasts such as Maleva and others, breasts were their big weakness and this was no different for Aurora.

"You're sucking so hard on my nipples! I'm about to come! Yes! I'm coming! I don't even remember the last time I felt like this! You're doing it! You're breaking the curse!" Aurora had a strong and erotic reaction to him making love to her. She was right, this was definitely working on her.

"Keep sucking on her breasts, Michael! It's working!" Maleva encouraged him, shouting in the small room.

*Please, work...* Michael hoped for the best

"The curse is being lifted! I'm feeling like myself again! This is working! I'm able to move like I used to again! And... And... I'm coming! I'm coming so hard!" Aurora moaned.

*Good thing because I'm going to... I need to pull out of her, it wouldn't be fair to her for me to cum inside of her during our first time together. Plus, this is only to help her break the curse...* the young man remembered right in the nick of time, pulling out of her before it was too late.

Both of them came at roughly the same time, Michael dumping his load all over Aurora's wondrous tits! Beautifully covering them!

Michael suddenly shifted into his wolf-boy form as he came simply because of how arousing this felt and how strongly he reacted to this massive orgasm.

"Michael, you've turned into your wolf form as you orgasmed..." Maleva pointed out to him.

"Uh?" he wasn't even certain how this came to be in the first place.

"You've become a wolf again. Good, because..." Aurora also noticed after the curse was lifted... However... He wasn't the only one who this happened to...

Michael and Maleva turned their heads back to the mature woman.

"... This just happened to me, as well. Thanks for lifting the curse for me, Michael-boy..." Aurora finished her sentence, but her voice turned much darker as she continued speaking.

Aurora had turned into a magnificent and fully-developed werewolf with ears, animalistic eyes, a long snout, sharp fangs, deadly claws, and a long tail and she even cultivated some wolf fur on some parts of her body, such as her arms. Her fur was of a snow-white color.

Aurora was not just any ordinary wolf, she was an Arctic wolf.

*She transformed! She's a werewolf, as well! Just like Maleva!*

"It's the first time you've completed your werewolf form in front of me, grandma. I had no idea you looked like this..." Maleva uttered, royally impressed by her grandma.

"There's always a first time for everything, right?" Aurora chuckled.

"You're a snow werewolf or something like that..." Michael mentioned.

"Yeah. Something like that..." Aurora grinned, enjoying the fact that she just transformed.

# Chapter 27: Ending The Big, Bad Wolf

The threat was right outside.

They didn't have much time to prepare.

As nightfall came and the full moon rose in the dark sky, it wasn't only Aurora who came prepared. She wasn't the only lady around here who so turned into a wolf as one was right at the door, waiting for the opportunity to strike, Maleva shifted into her werewolf form, as well.

This bestial and erotic pheromone in the air was spreading like a virus in the room and in the rest of the cabin. First, Michael transformed upon dumping his thick load all over Aurora's big tits, then, his childhood friend, Maleva did, as well. During his wild transformation, the young man also finished into his full werewolf stage. He no longer looked like a wolf boy, but instead like a bipedal monstrous dog.

Everyone had turned and everyone was getting ready to receive that one undesired guest, who they could smell right outside, lurking around Aurora's wooden cabin.

"Not bad for your werewolf form..." The lusty and horny Aurora smirked and purred as she laid eyes on Michael's final form for the first time.

"Grandma. We should probably focus on the task at hand right now. The menace is right there outside," Maleva cut her off, profoundly thinking the moment wasn't exactly right. She was also becoming a bit jealous of her because of all the attention she was giving to her friend, but she couldn't let that be too apparent, so everyone noticed.

"Yeah. You're probably right, Maleva..." She looked the other way and pretended not to be staring at this monster that was Michael and his remarkable muscles.

"Right. What should we do now? What's our strategy? I don't like being trapped in here. I feel like it's a terrible mistake. We should be out there, hunting this thing that did this to you, grandma!" Maleva, the youngest huntress of the village, was adamant about this point. According to her, they were sitting ducks in Aurora's cabin.

"Um... Interesting..." Aurora purred, "And this menace out there is the same rogue wolf that you mentioned earlier, the one that nearly ended your lives not too long ago, right?" Aurora asked the two of them.

"Right," Maleva nodded, exhausted from being prowled upon by the shadow werewolf.

"Ma'am. I agree with Maleva. We should be out there fighting, Not hiding," The male in the room made his intentions very clear. It was two against one at this point. Even if she was to be against their plan, they would still go ahead with it, anyway, so there was no point in arguing about it now.

"So, I guess we have already decided on our tactic, then," Aurora announced.

***

Everyone rushed outside the wooden cabin in the middle of the woods.

The final confrontation against the rogue shadow werewolf was soon about to take place.

However, Michael, Maleva, and Aurora needed to find it first. They needed to track it down. They needed to hunt it.

A new hunt was about to take place.

The three wolves used their smelling abilities to track the threat in the surrounding area. The three of them could perfectly see in the dark, but their smell was going to be their greatest ally in this battle. Wherever the menace was, they were going to hunt it until it was dealt with. This could be dangerous though, so the three of them desperately had to be careful if they didn't want to fall tonight.

Michael and Maleva took the lead. They patrolled the sector while Aurora stayed a bit more behind, staying in support in case something really bad ever happened. The moon shone brightly in the sky as the two young wolves ran side-by-side on all fours. Running and behaving like actual wolves and nothing like humans.

"I detect something over there in that direction!" werewolf Michael communicated to Maleva as he shook his head to the right. The two ventured as deep as they could into the woods surrounding Aurora's home.

"That's where the lake is at... Are you sure...?" Maleva questioned his judgment, not belittling him, of course, but suspecting that he might be wrong because he wasn't as used to hunting as she was.

"Completely certain. It's the same entity we have been battling this entire time. It's at the lake," he swore to her.

...

"Then, that's exactly where we need to go. It's probably leading us there, though. We have to be careful," Maleva pointed out to him.

"Come!" Michael abruptly changed direction to the right and headed toward the lake.

Maleva followed.

***

In only a few minutes, the pair of wolves came down to the lake while Aurora stayed behind. They chose to hunt in the woods while they went to the lake. She chose to support them from a distance, but the truth was that the two much younger wolves outraced her so much that there was no way that she was actually able to keep up with them. They were much faster than Aurora, the veteran wolf.

The bright moon in the dark sky reflected on the lake at night. Michael and Maleva were there.

"You were right, Michael, this was a great idea to come here, its smell is much stronger here. It's got to be here," Maleva admitted as she searched around the place, desperately hunting their enemy down.

Where was it?

"I'll be honest with you, I no longer have any idea if this was the right call to come here or not."

"What makes you say that?" she turned to him.

"I don't think we're the ones who are hunting it, but it might just be hunting us, instead," he pointed out to her.

"Why? What do you mean?"

"Over there!" Maleva looked into the distance where her childhood friend indicated to her: Then, she saw it for the first time, the rogue and shadow werewolf, whose body was still covered in dead leaves, was staring right at them.

"It's here," Michael declared.

"It sure is the case. But it should be fine. They're standing on that tiny island at the center of the lake. It should be no problem for us. They can't get out of there, really. We're safe. They're not hunting us, really," Naturally, Maleva spoke a bit too fast right there, because of a gust of wind later and...

... It was now right behind them. The shadow wolf seemingly had teleported right behind them!

"Mal!"

First up, the enemy sneak attacked Maleva in her back, violently clawing her. Attacking her so fast and so strongly that she almost immediately came down to her knees.

"Huh..." how could Maleva, the huntress, be defeated so easily?

"No!"

Then, it was Michael's turn.

The young man was so confused by this sudden attack that he didn't guard himself in time before the rogue werewolf struck again. The enemy turned to him and swung at him, clawing his chest with both claws.

"Ugh!"

Michael also came down to the ground, defeated.

The shadow werewolf covered in dead leaves stood above the both of them.

"I told you I was going to take all the Moonlit Sins for myself," The dark voice was cool, precise, and collected.

# Chapter 28: We Hunt In Pack

It truly felt like everything was over.

Michael was down.

Maleva was also.

The situation was pretty dire as the shadow werewolf covered in dead Autumn leaves stepped right between the two hunters. It towered over them. Triumphant.

"Mal... Run..." the young man begged her to run away and to save her own life while he tried to do something to keep the beast occupied while she escaped.

"No way... No way that I'm leaving you behind..." she replied.

"What are you doing? Are you nuts? I'm no one and you're one of the Moonlit Sins. You're far more important than I am. Far more important than I'll ever be, in fact," he argued with her.

"Don't say things like that..." Maleva never thought of herself as too important either, to begin with, but she felt awful for her childhood friend who personally thought his life was worthless. She didn't think it was the case, at all...

"Michael…"

"As much as I feel horrible to interrupt your final moment, I won't kill you right this second, there's something I need to show the both of you first," the shadow werewolf declared to them.

"What? What are you talking about? Take me and let her go," Michael shouted at the creature.

"No… Let him go…" Maleva insisted.

"Shut up the two of you!" the rogue werewolf snarled as he violently picked the two of them up and blinked out of existence! Ran so fast across the water of the lake that it felt like it was teleporting!

*Boom!*

The shadow werewolf dropped the two hunters on the ground. They were now on that small island at the center of the lake. They had been taken away from the beach where they were a second ago. As soon as their bodies were dumped on the ground, Michael and Maleva were shown a bunch of rocks at the center of the island. No. They were not only rocks. They were sculptures made of stone. Altars. Michael and Maleva were both shocked to discover that there were eight sculptures in total.

All of them were altars of wolves.

Each one of them was sculpted slightly differently and all of them had different color variations ranging from golden, bronze, silver, copper, and more... However, seven of the altars surrounded one of them in particular. One that was onyx and that showed a wolf man who reassembled Michael a lot with his longer hair, which covered half his face.

"What is all of this?" The young man asked.

"It's us..." Maleva admitted.

"Oh, so you know what these altars are after all?" the dead leaves-covered werewolf taunted her.

"It's us? What do you mean?" Michael couldn't understand at first. But then...

*Wait! Seven wolves are surrounding this dude? This has to be representing the seven Moonlit Deadly Sins, but who's that in the middle? It looks like a half-man, half-beast...*

"Let me guess. It's all the Moonlit Sins, right?" Michael suspected before she could even explain this to her.

"That's right... It's all of us..." Maleva confirmed.

"Do you know why I wished to show you all of this, Micahel?" the shadow werewolf interrogated him.

"I don't know. Is it because you want to share your love and passion for rock sculpting or something?" Michael still found a way to make a joke out of this horrible and deadly situation.

"You had to see this because I wished to demonstrate to you that you'll never become the beast master that you could have been—you'll never become the Moonlit Master you should have been. You can already forget about uniting the seven deadly sins because I am going to be the one to do it instead of you. Starting with Maleva right here," the dead leaves-covered nemesis carefully explained to him.

"I am not going to let you do this!" Michael was furious to hear that their plan was still to take Maleva for themselves, as well as the rest of the sins. Even though, no one knew who they were at the moment.

"It's too late now. It's time for you to die, Michael!"

"Noooo!" Maleva never wanted her childhood friend to be killed, but she couldn't move. Her body was aching too much. She still tried moving to save him, but she was too slow.

The shadow werewolf was right about to stomp on the man's skull and violently murder him when all of a sudden...

The water surrounding the small island at the center of the lake began getting frozen. Bit by bit, the water turned icy almost as if the wind was changing and that it was suddenly turning Winter all of a sudden. Snow started to slowly fall in the sky. Everything around them became of a solstice white and blue color temperature and it all turned chilly.

"Hum...?" Michael was shocked he was still alive after the shadow werewolf abruptly stopped right before he could finish stomping on his head.

"What is all this ice?" Maleva asked herself.

"This can't..." the dead leaves-covered beast could be heard, uttering to themselves.

Soon enough, the entire lake turned to ice.

"Thought we were hunting as a pack?" Then, her voice was heard on the other side of the lake. Aurora's voice.

Aurora showed up!

Still in her arctic werewolf form, she rushed at the dead leaves-covered werewolf. Icy spikes came with her and were thrown by her right at the face of the shadow werewolf.

The ice spikes violently hit their enemy in the chest, which was not enough to defeat it, but was indeed more than enough to distract it. This distracted him well enough, so Maleva could sneak up behind it.

"Yah!" Maleva, the huntress slashed its back, hurting him even more.

"My turn!" Then, the last ingredient needed to make this some killer teamwork, Michael came into the picture, as well. He jumped back to his feet, grabbed one of the ice spikes that Aurora had brought on land, and used it like a sword! Slashing his way and cutting the enemy's chest in one frosty swing! It was still snowing all over them as this battle raged on. The three pack members stood all around the shadow werewolf, Michael and Maleva barely standing but still standing.

The monster finally and slowly came down to its knees.

They had defeated it.

"We did it..." Maleva murmured.

"I can't believe we won..." Michael tiredly mentioned.

"Glad I found you two again before it was too late..." Aurora was happy these two were still alive to tell the tale.

"Um... Right... Thanks for that, Aurora... I mean, ma'am..." Michael scratched the back of his head.

"Now that we vanquished it, it should transform back into a human anytime now..." Maleva theorized...

However, that didn't happen. Instead, the seemingly deceased body slowly faded and turned into stone after it had been defeated. It turned into the same type of stone that all the sculptures on the tiny island were made of.

"You were saying?" Michael asked her, shocked by what he had just witnessed.

"... Or its body is going to turn into stone. I've never seen that before. Grandma! Have you ever seen that before?" She quickly sought Aurora for help.

"Um..."

Aurora squinted her eyes.

# Chapter 29: Aurora's Cabin

Everyone came back to Aurora's cabin in the woods as they brought the shadow wolf's body with them. The shadow werewolf's deceased and rocky body had been left on a long table in the shed not too far from Aurora's home. Only a couple of trees and a few feet of snow separated her house and the shed. Winter had truly come at last. There wasn't any snow out before they left for their midnight hunt. Aurora was the only reason as to why there was snow in the first place. Her presence and her transformation into her werewolf form caused all of this to happen. Without forgetting to mention that her battling their prey at the lake quickly shifted the regular snowfall into a storm.

Because that was exactly what it was right here outside: It was a violent storm.

However, thankfully, the three of them were back in Aurora's warm and cozy home in the middle of the forest.

In no time, they started the fireplace, and smoke was coming out of the chimney. There was going to be a nice and delicious meal following their perilous and challenging hunt—and the food Michael was going to have was no other than Aurora herself.

"Oh. Michel-honey! Do you mind giving me a hand in the living room?" The MILF with the snow-white hair asked him from the other room as the young man was still in the middle of setting the table for everyone as he truly thought they were going to have a regular supper. But this wasn't what Aurora had in store for them at all.

Everyone was back in their human forms again.

When Michael came into the living room, joining Aurora after being asked to come here, he came face-to-face with the snow-white-haired MILF as she was sitting on a red couch with her thighs curved behind her head. The MILF was showing off everything to Michael.

Aurora was almost entirely naked other than three strategically placed cherry-red ribbons that could be seen on both of her nipples and on her pussy. Otherwise, without these three red ribbons, she'd be all exposed for him, which was almost already the case.

Michael's cheeks turned red hot as soon as he stepped into the living room and discovered Aurora like this. Maleva was still setting the table up in the other room when he was so kindly invited to join into the living room. The young huntress knew nothing of this.

"Aurora? What are you doing?"

"Michael."

"Maleva," but it was too late to stop anything now. By the time the young huntress penetrated into the living room, it was pretty much already a done deal. Her grandma had already seduced the young boy in heat and he had already undone the three red ribbons erotically displayed on her voluptuous body. Starting with the two ribbons where her nipples were.

*Boing! Boing!*

Her tits and more specifically her nipples had been freed! Finally revealed to the young man!

Then, he undid the third and final ribbon, as well. The one that was covering her private part between her legs. Aurora's pussy had finally been revealed once more to him and this was such a glorious moment for him.

Her pussy was simply perfect. Gorgeous in every way. Something that was pretty interesting about her was the fact that she had a trimmed snow-white bush, which made this part of her body even more magnificent. Her snow-white hair went perfectly with her pink pussy lips.

Michael was unable to resist.

The young boy hugged her with his shaft surfing right on top of her pussy as he fondled her breasts and placed his face right between her gigantic marshmallows! However, surfing on the exterior of her pussy was far from being enough. *Woosh!* The boy slid his cock deep inside of Aurora and began making love to her!

The last time Michael had sex with her it was to save her soul, but there was nothing to save her. This was only for pleasure. This was also how and when Aurora truly revealed herself to the young man.

Aurora—the Arctic wolf was definitely a Moonlit Sin.

She was without a shadow of a doubt Gluttony.

Her granddaughter was lusty, the grandmother was no other than Gluttony. A perfect sex glutton.

"Everything I heard about you was true, grandma..."

"Maleva! This isn't what you're thinking! I simply wanted to have a bit more of him before our meal! That's all!" Aurora promised her.

"So, you're having a meal before the actual meal?" Maleva questioned him. The young huntress with the red and green hair was furious that she went behind her back and was having sex with Michael again. This time, there was no point to it. It was only for sex and the problem was that Aurora was recently fucked by Michael.

The sex glutton was working her magic. She couldn't contain herself whenever she was around Michael. This lusty feeling inside of her grew even stronger when she was alone with the young man, which had recently been the case in the living room...

Could Maleva be jealous of her ancestor right now?

She could be seen blushing as Michael went to town with Aurora's pussy. He wouldn't stop pumping his big dick in and out of her at light speed. Aurora was exactly what the young boy needed. A nice, wet pussy, which perfectly enveloped itself around his cock. It felt like her tight pussy was sucking his member inward, sucking it inside. Almost as if Aurora never wished to let his cock go. Ever.

"Oh! Aw! You're about to make me come!" Michael's dick was Aurora's weakness. She couldn't help but be embraced by a powerful orgasm nearly as soon as she was dicked by him.

Then, as he gave this mesmerizing and animalistic orgasm, Aurora quickly shifted back into the arctic wolf that she always was. Fangs. Claws. Wolf's ears. Her eyes changed, as well. She turned back into a werewolf.

"I'm also cumming!" It was Michael's turn.

"It's okay. I'm way past my time to have kids. You can shoot your big load inside of me..." she moaned.

"I may?" This excited him even more somehow and he moved faster, triggering him to cum and fill her up ever so slightly before he was originally expected to.

"Aw..."

As Michael dumped his load inside of her pussy, he was then the one who shifted into a wolf as well. It was his turn. Now, both of them had become werewolves again. Everything happened as Maleva watched in pure, constant, and tortured arousal.

# Chapter 30: Michael's Pack

Outside, the moon shone bright again in the infinite darkness of the woods.

The only one among the three who still had to turn was Maleva. It was two wolves on one human.

Aurora held her granddaughter in the woods surrounding the cabin while Michael in his werewolf form could have his way with her. Maleva subjected absolutely no opposition to this other than feeling pretty uncomfortable regarding the fact that her grandma was basically using her.

This was a completely uncharted territory for her and their family. Their family would never have sex together, but everything was different now for some reason. Everything had become different with Michael involved.

"Owwwwwllll!" Michael howled at the moon.

"Owwmnwnlll!" Aurora did, as well.

"I've never been more wet than now..." Maleva finally admitted to herself out loud. With her long legs completely wide open, she personally realized just how much her succulent pussy was so dripping wet...

Being a perverted wolf right now, Michael leaned forward, his long tongue gushing out of his mouth before he swung it around to lick her delicious pussy all over. Starting from her pink clitoris to the end of her pussy lips, not too far from where her butt-hole resided.

Declaring Maleva overwhelmed would have been a total understatement. With Michael licking her pussy, getting it even wetter than before, and Aurora holding her from behind, playing with her young, big tits, Maleva was clearly the center of attention at the moment.

"Thank you for bringing such a nice young man into my home," Aurora took the time to thank her granddaughter for this. The truth was that it had been forever since the last time Aurora had anyone at her place. She resided in the further region of the woods. Farther away from everywhere Michael had ever been before.

Tonight, because of Aurora's snow wolf abilities, there was a strong wind in the air as well as lots of snow. It was snowing even more than it was the case before at the lake during the showdown with the enemy.

"It's not like I brought him to you or anything like that, Grandma! He's my friend, you know?" she reminded her.

"Yeah, and that's exactly why he's eating your pussy right now."

"Grandma! You can't say things like that!" the young woman raged at Aurora for even saying something like that in the first place, even though that was the absolute truth.

However, the fact of the matter was that eating her pussy was only the very beginning of him using her.

Michael's werewolf cock was throbbing in the moonlight. Maleva saw it as the creature pulled back from her. An instant later the beast had already found his way inside of her.

*Smoosh!*

The male wolf was fucking Maleva. Sexually dominating with the passion and rage of a serious up-and-coming werewolf alpha leader. We shall see, but Michael was definitely on track to become a real pack leader who could lead his own harem. Perhaps he was moving too fast, but he had already in mind that Aurora was part of his pack, even though absolutely nothing was certain yet.

"Owwoollll!" It was now Maleva's time to howl as she shifted into her wolf side, finally joining the others. The sexual pleasure she had been subjected to by Michael had made this possible. She turned into her real self because of him. He only gave her the final push she needed.

"Good girl!" Aurora soon congratulated her.

This was right before the MILF brought her big werewolf tits right on top of Maleva's skull and squished her with them.

*Thump! Thump!*

These loud and heavy noises could be heard as the MILF's tits were slammed right on top of her head. This didn't really hurt her too much, but she clearly felt it as her breasts hit her. Now, they were being maintained right on top of her head, squishing her, beautifully squishing her.

"There. They're for you," Aurora announced to the male werewolf.

Michael understood what Aurora's tits were for pretty quickly: They were for sucking and that was the exact reason as to why they had been set free all over Maleva's skull. Aurora wanted him to take her tits into his mouth, which he soon did.

"Hey, what do you think you're doing?" Maleva argued with Aurora for a while before the male wolf came closer. Slapping and hitting Maleva's pussy even stronger with his bestial dick as he leaned forward to have better access to his buffet right here. Treating Aurora's breasts like prey, he targeted them both at the same time and managed to bring both of her nipples deep in his mouth as he feasted on them, sucking on them all he wanted.

"Hmmhh..." this made Aurora moan in no time...

"Owwwwll!"

"Oowwwwooll!"

"Oeewwwoolll!"

The three wolves then howled at the moon.

The moment during which the male werewolf was going to ejaculate inside of his female had arrived.

Michael kept swaying his hips back and forth as he copulated with her. Still sucking on Aurora's thick nipples at the same time as he fucked her.

"He's cumming! He's cumming inside of me! I'm coming too! I'm coming so hard, Michael!" Maleva shouted in pure exhaustion, panic, and pleasure. All of her sexual frustrations left her body and she became anew again.

"Let it all out, sweetheart," Aurora gently patted her head with her huge, ultra-comforting, heavy breasts.

Hoping to make the young girl feel even more at peace and comfortable, Aurora slid her right palm down to her belly after passing through her breasts, touching them quite a bit before reaching her belly.

"Umm..."

She held her belly pretty tight with the palm of her hand.

This was when she sensed something inside of her...

"You're pregnant," Aurora announced merely a handful of seconds after first touching her belly.

\*\*\*

Meanwhile, in the shed not too far from Aurora's cabin the stone body of the shadow werewolf had been left.

Without anyone being present to tell the tale, the stone began cracking. Deep fissures appeared all over the petrified body of the werewolf until the person inside could attempt to come out... Something was definitely still alive inside...

The shadow werewolf wasn't dead.

It was still very much alive and it did everything it could to come out. It attempted to hatch out of its petrified and frozen body as if it was an egg.

The creature wished to soon walk out of the shed. Hoping to burst through the wooden doors and then walk in the cold snow... But whatever was inside of this frozen cocoon had to hatch out of it first in order to do that...

The shadow werewolf was still hanging on for dear life...

\*\*\*

The task they had been given had been completed.

Michael and Maleva had gone into the woods, met with Aurora, handed her the parcel, and moved on.

So, a few more things happened to the three of them in the woods including lots of sex and a final confrontation with the shadow werewolf, making the most pleasant visit, minus the battles and all.

Michael and Maleva both came back to Cherrywood to report to the huntress's mother.

The rocky, petrified body of the shadow werewolf was brought to the village, as well.

"So, we were recently able to examine the rock-hard body you brought home, and whoever or whatever was inside, it's definitely dead. There's no chance it's still alive," the mother confirmed to them both, yet, there was something that was slightly different now that was not the case before, there was a cut in the back of the rock. As if it had been opened after having been brought back to the village.

The petrified body was hollow, which was not the case before.

Michael and Maleva didn't notice that.

"However, let me recap some of this a bit... So, I sent you to bring a simple parcel to your grandmother and you get in trouble with that big, bad wolf again?" Maleva's mother stood angered with both arms folded together.

"Mom..."

"No, this is not what you think, ma'am! This isn't Maleva's fault! It was me! I was the one who put your daughter in danger! Please don't punish her for this!" Michael didn't want his new girlfriend to get into any trouble.

The mother turned to the young man.

Her frown quickly turned into a smile.

"Now, that's very kind of you to try to help my daughter, but I'm rather certain you did everything you could on this trip to protect her. I'm sure you did great, boy. I'm proud of you. Thanks for accompanying my daughter for this job," Tears almost appeared inside of the mother's eyes as she only thought good things about the boy.

"Ah... It's-it's nothing, really..." Michael scratched the back of his head, not knowing what to say or do.

"Aaaaaaannnnddd... During all this time, I kept track of these two and watched over them!" Lycanna suddenly appeared out of nowhere and placed herself between Michael and Maleva.

"Hey! That's not true! Grandmother told us you had secretly been staying in her house the entire time and ate all of her sweets!" Maleva confronted the short wolf girl with sheer fire and passion.

"That's not true..." she lied to them as she began sweating...

"Don't lie, Lycanna. Aurora told us everything already," Even Michael was absolutely certain she did it.

"What? Did she really tell you, guys?" Lycanna was trapped. She was done for.

"She did!"

"She did!"

Michael and Maleva both shouted to her at the same time!

Meanwhile, Maleva's mother giggled...

"These three make for a dynamic duo..." the mother murmured to herself.

# Afterword

Thanks for purchasing this book.

Getting this book ready and finished was a lot of work, but it paid off in the end.

Of course, I don't want to bore you with this afterword and the why and the how to how this erotic and strange novel came about... However, I'd just like to say that the origins of this book began with the idea of doing something *werewolf-themed.*

Dah!

Right?

Can I possibly be more obvious? In all seriousness, the original concept for this project was for me to write something that would be a hundred percent for me. An original idea that I would be delighted to work on every day for as long as necessary to complete the project, no matter how many weeks or months it took. I personally adore werewolves and their mythologies and everything about them, so I decided to add my own spin to it.

Naturally, I wished for the novel to be erotic.

So, that's how an erotic werewolf book came about and to be honest, I firmly believe the two of them work well together... Erotica and the werewolf genre. That doesn't mean I made it work in my novel, but I sure hope you were entertained a bit at the very least.

Special thanks to Logy, my editor and proofreader, who stuck with me the entire time I worked on that book. Without you my friend, it would not have been the same. Your encouragement, feedback, and proofreading meant so much to me.

Another special thanks to Jim (JimJim's Renders) who helped me a ton during the inception of the project and pretty much convinced me that the chosen title was the right one. Thanks for all your help and encouragement.

Thanks to all the artists who contributed to the project. Without all of you, this publishing process wouldn't be anywhere near as fun.

Thank you to everyone in my life who supports me and my work.

Thank you.

—Camille Juteau.

# Credits

Story By: Camille Juteau

Proofreader: Logy Hebdon

Illustration By: TigerDrop


Title Logo Artist: IvanMichael12

# More Copyrights

ISBN Numbers
ISBN Number For e-book (Electronic Book) version:
978-1-7782777-3-3

ISBN Number For Paperback (Physical) version:

978-1-7782777-2-6

Camille Juteau